The Secret of the Sleigh Bell

The Legend of Bell Mountain

written and illustrated by

Eddie Davenport

iUniverse, Inc.
New York   Bloomington

The Secret of the Sleigh Bell
The Legend of Bell Mountain

iUniverse books may be ordered through booksellers or by contacting:

iUniverse
1663 Liberty Drive
Bloomington, IN 47403
www.iuniverse.com
1-800-Authors (1-800-288-4677)

Because of the dynamic nature of the Internet, any Web addresses or links contained in this book may have changed since publication and may no longer be valid. The views expressed in this work are solely those of the author and do not necessarily reflect the views of the publisher, and the publisher hereby disclaims any responsibility for them.

ISBN: 978-1-4502-5700-8 (sc)
ISBN: 978-1-4502-5701-5 (dj)
ISBN: 978-1-4502-5702-2 (ebook)

Printed in the United States of America

iUniverse rev. date: 09/03/2010

Acknowledgements

This book is dedicated to all those who are young at heart.

Thanks go to Lonnie Howell, and Ed & Kate Goliak, who donated countless hours in reading and critiquing the manuscript.

Special thanks go to Wendy Stacy, my childhood friend, whose artistic abilities inspired the front cover design.

A special thanks and love to my Mom, Ilse Davenport. Without her love and unyielding support this book would not be possible.

Prologue

Ten-year-old Aspen Pepin shivered as he stood in the snow, his stomach growling. Night was closing in on New Hampshire's Wapack Mountain Range. Not knowing which way to go, he stood silently, intently listening, watching the snow fall to the ground, with his attention now on the sparkling speckles of icy stardust.

"That's where the sparkles come from, you know, the stars," Aspen said to Oreo, his small dog tucked into his down-filled oversized red jacket. The dimming light gave way to the rising full moon, turning the white snow a beautiful pale, cool blue. Cold as it was, Aspen appreciated the mystical beauty of winter and all its offerings. Snowflakes descended, ever so softly, so quietly, so beautifully.

"It's all good," he whispered into Oreo's ear.

Oreo

Oreo, a stray puppy, had the good fortune of having been abandoned at Windblown Animal Shelter, located at the base of Monadnock Mountain, on the morning of October twenty-third. Aspen and his father, Topher Pepin, arrived only moments after the opening of the shelter with their weekly donations of pet food and an ample supply of biscuits for the dogs. Topher felt that the freedom to make choices should be part of Aspen's life lessons. One of those choices was how to spend his weekly allowance. Aspen never spent all of it on himself. Instead of buying toys, he bought food for his homeless friends at the shelter. Aspen's priority was always the same: to visit the older dogs first.

"They looked the saddest and they needed loving most of all," Aspen would say when asked why he made his rounds in that order. Moments like this reminded him of how lucky he was to have his own family, home, and friends.

Even at the young age of ten, he had a keen sense of gratitude for what he had, always wishing the best in life for everyone and everything. "Thank you," he would often say aloud to no one in particular.

"What's all this red glitter doing all over the lobby floor?" asked Topher, when he arrived that morning.

"We have a new guest at the shelter," Mrs. Ogohre answered, "and apparently quite a mischievous little one. She found her way into the closet and into the basket of craft supplies. I just had to laugh at her."

As Aspen made his way from cage to cage, he noticed a trail of glitter coming to an end in front of a holding cage for new arrivals. When he saw the little dog for the first time, he giggled. She was white and covered with large, black spots that reminded him of Oreo cookies with an extra sprinkling of red jimmies. She didn't look like a stray; she was clean and well groomed except for the glitter. He became silent, watching the little dog tilt her head to one side, Aspen then mimicking the move. They continued their game for a while, playfully sizing each other up.

Topher noticed the interaction. The look on his son's face gave him the impression that Aspen might recognize her. *That's odd,* Topher thought.

Aspen smiled and stuck his finger through the wire screen. The little dog wagged its white bushy tail and licked Aspen's fingers.

Topher had an inkling that this meeting between Aspen and the dog was more than a chance encounter. He stroked the side of his face, thinking, contemplating an idea. Thirty minutes later, his idea came to fruition and the adoption of the little dog was complete. Aspen and his new companion, now officially named Oreo, were on their way home. That's how Oreo came to live in the Wapack Mountains near Bell Mountain Village.

Bell Mountain Village

Long ago, when New Hampshire was first explored by settlers, they often heard what they thought were sounds of sleigh bells in the distant mountains. Over the years, many of them looked for the source of the enchanting sound, but nothing was ever found. It was like the solemn call of a loon echoing from nearby Cranberry Pond—something that could be heard but not always seen. The settlers took this as a good sign, settled in the valley, and named their little town Bell Mountain Village.

The Pepin's home was a twenty-minute ride up the western slope from the village. On calm, autumn nights, music from the Kidder Mountain Oompah Band could be heard echoing up through the valley as they played lively waltzes from the Adirondack-style gazebo in the town square. The wood-shingled homes in the village were stucco and painted white. In traditional European style, hearts and tulips accented the painted fronts. Below the windows hung flower boxes filled with blooming red, white, and pink geraniums. Park benches were scattered along the brick-lined sidewalks, and the streets were paved with cobblestones. The old storefront windows were decorated with pumpkins, dried maple leaves of many colors, and scarecrows stuffed with hay and dressed in worn-out overalls, faded flannel shirts, and straw hats riddled with holes. Flyers announcing the upcoming Pumpkin Fair in nearby Keene were taped to some of the doors.

The Pepins enjoyed the distant views from their mountaintop home. A short walk through a perennial patch of orange daisies, red daylilies, and purple gay fellows opened onto a sloping green pasture, where hay was grown in the summer. Pine, oak, maple, and birch trees edged the pasture and continued into the distant mountains. To one side of the perennial patch was a small knoll, and upon it, an old wooden park bench. In the evening, the soft illumination of gas lanterns lining the village's town square could be seen.

Oreo's New Home

Oreo had forgotten her temporary housing arrangement at Windblown Animal Shelter by the end of her bumpy ride home in the back of Topher's rickety, old pickup truck. Oreo instinctively positioned herself with her two front paws over the edge of the pickup truck's rail bed, firmly planting her back paws against the metal frame of the bed. She braced herself for the onslaught of rushing wind against her face.

Aspen held on tightly to her new pink collar, a gift from the shelter. They both reveled in distinctive autumn sights and aromas that only old country roads could provide. Aspen smiled as he watched Oreo with her nose in the wind and ears flapping like the wings of a sparrow. Apparently, a few bugs in her eyes were worth the thrill of the ride. Red glitter mix with dust settled on the dirt road as the truck sped out of view.

At the edge of Contoocook Frog Pond, a bull moose raised his well-adorned rack of antlers from the dark water. Weeds hung from them like tinsel on a Christmas tree. The moose was enjoying a much-needed afternoon plunge in the cool water of the pond to ward off annoying horse flies and to gorge on pondweed and water lilies. It was not intimidated or disturbed by the noise of Topher's old truck, with its rusted out exhaust pipes amplifying the sounds of the sputtering engine. In fact, it looked forward to the occasional human interaction.

Topher wondered how the enormous moose managed to survive hunting season every year, boldly grazing at the water's edge in plain view. The locals nicknamed the moose Guardian, figuring it must have a guardian angel keeping it out of harm's way.

The noisy truck continued down the road until it reached a gravel driveway, where it came to a dusty stop in front of a stone house. Annie looked up from her fenced-in perennial garden where she was planting tulip bulbs for next spring's awakening.

"Hi, Mom," Aspen yelled as he spotted her. He hopped out of the truck and reached back, picking up Oreo and setting her on the ground. Immediately she ran up the old, worn brick sidewalk, and through the open gate of the white picket fence that was in need of a few nails and a fresh coat of paint. Ears flopping in the wind, bushy tail high, she ran straight into the arms of Annie, offering wet kisses on her cheek, which Annie reluctantly accepted.

"Oh my, who's this?" Annie asked, giggling as Oreo continued her wet assault. She saw the smiles on Aspen and Topher's faces and knew instantly that this little dog might be a permanent guest.

Aspen cheerfully replied. "This is my new friend, and her name is Oreo, just like the cookie."

Topher smiled as he thought how easy it was going to be to win Annie over. After all, she was outnumbered three to one.

Annie wiped her hands on her white pocketed apron then fidgeted with her hair making sure the braids were still tightly rolled into buns on either side of her head.

Annie gave Topher a disapproving look that quickly evaporated when she saw how happy her little boy was. She laughed. "Okay, she can stay, but she needs a bath," and without hesitation headed toward the potting shed. "Bring Oreo with you Aspen."

Although Oreo looked clean, Annie quickly concluded that Oreo might as well get used to baths now if she was going to live inside their home. She prepared a sudsy bath in the old, chipped porcelain bathtub that was kept behind the potting shed. Oreo was not too happy about her new situation and made feeble attempts to escape from the sudsy water, but she soon relented at the sound of Annie's soothing humming.

Cluck, the resident red-tailed rooster, crowed from the top of the henhouse as he watched the scene unfold. He had no instinctual sense of time, crowing whenever the mood hit him or whenever he wanted to be noticed. He crowed excitedly, announcing the new arrival to the Pepins clan.

After a quick towel drying and a few crunchy treats, Oreo acquainted herself to the inside surroundings of her new home. She located a perfect spot to call her own on the warm braided rug that lay in front of the stone fireplace. Oreo heaved a heavy sigh as she settled in. As she lay there embracing the warmth of the fire, she had an uneasy feeling of being watched. She lifted her head turning to see where this uneasy feeling was emanating from, and she found herself face to face with Scruff the cat. With their noses only one inch apart, Scruff voiced a loud "meow."

Scruff didn't acquire his name for being handsome; in fact, he looked as mean as any cat you would see on Halloween night. He had come to the family a few years earlier. Annie had gone to the mailbox to retrieve the mail left by Divi, the postman. The oversized mailbox had lost its door after being sideswiped by the county snowplow truck, and Annie often left slices of banana bread, cupcakes, or some other offerings of friendship there. Divi always stopped when he saw the red flag in its upward position, knowing the red flag didn't always indicate there was outgoing mail.

On that day, Annie had walked down the driveway, avoiding the potholes left by the mud season, to make her usual deposits in the mailbox. It was then that she saw the cat for the first time. Caked up with dried road grime, it snarled and wrinkled its forehead as it peered at Annie with squinted green eyes. Annie ran back to the house, dropping tiny packages in the mud.

"Topher, there's a wild, scruffy animal in our mailbox!" she screamed. The mangy cat looked more pitiful than any barnyard cat Annie had ever seen. Other than an old leather collar, there was nothing in which to identify him. Annie took pity on the smelly, muddy cat. It took a while for the cat to trust her, but Scruff soon became one of Annie's prized possessions.

Independent Scruff wasn't the fighting kind of cat, and he used his sixteen pounds, several more than Oreo weighed, in other ways to get his point across. This particular spot on the rug was his, and he wasn't going to let this newcomer think otherwise. Meowing, Scruff attempted to sit on top of Oreo, forcing her off his spot. Oreo settled on the top of the couch from where she could keep a watchful eye out for the green-eyed beast. She refused to be humiliated by that fat, green-eyed cat.

That evening the Pepins gathered in the back yard on the knoll that overlooked the valley, Bell Mountain Village nestled within. The scenic view was beautiful now with autumn foliage at its peak and crowning rows of apple trees speckled with bright red dotting the distant hills. Annie and Topher sat on the old wooden bench watching Aspen and Oreo play together, chasing chipmunks around rows of neatly stacked firewood.

Cluck hid in the tall grass executing random surprise attacks on Scruff. They were often seen chasing each other; it was a most unusual friendship for a cat and rooster.

It had been a wonderful autumn day, full of laughter and play. Aspen knew this little dog would soon become his best buddy.

The Chase

Right before Christmas, snow fell peacefully, blanketing the ground. Awakening to the smell of brewing coffee and hickory-smoked bacon, Aspen sat up on the edge of his bed, rubbed his eyes, and focused on the window. Snow had collected in the corners of each windowpane. He could see immediately that it was a perfect day for sledding.

For Oreo, it would also be a perfect day; she loved snow-hopping. Aspen hurriedly ate and thanked Annie for breakfast, and then headed toward the rear door, Oreo right behind him. Aspen always took advantage of any opportunity to go sledding, and Christmas Eve was no exception. In the mudroom, he laced up his oversized boots, threw on his red, fluffy winter jacket, and then hurried out the back door. He stopped at the brick-colored barn on his way to the snow-covered pasture to pick up Easy Slider, his favorite sledding shovel. Oreo, not far behind him, made a game of jumping into the large impressions in the snow made by Aspen's boots.

At the top of the hill was a small planting of pine, leafless birch, and maple trees that gave backdrop to brightly painted bird feeders and multi-roomed birdhouses nailed to weathered fence posts. Topher had planted the small grouping of trees for Annie when they first moved into their mountain home. She always said that even on the cloudiest of days, her feathered friends could see the bright colors and find their way home. Annie would often sing, "Paint them bright and happy, and bright and happy thy guests will be."

Oreo didn't notice the snow pom-poms collecting on her fur as she jumped from footprint to footprint; she simply enjoyed being a free spirit, having fun, and most of all, being with her best friend Aspen.

Toboggans, wooden sleds with metal runners, and large red plastic saucers that resembled oversized garbage can lids were the most common means of downhill sledding in the Wapack Mountain Range, but for Aspen the best way was on Easy Slider. Sometimes, with Oreo tucked inside his jacket, he would slide down the steep embankment of the knoll, and then to the distant edge of the sloping meadow. That was the fun part; climbing back up was not. Often, Oreo preferred a free ride back by sitting in the wide shovel as Aspen dragged it behind him.

At the top of the knoll, Aspen sat on Easy Slider with the handle between his legs, which he used as a steering rod. "Weeeeee," Aspen yelled, as he pushed against the snow with his hands beginning his descent. Faster and faster, down the hill he went, pretending he was competing in a downhill bobsledding race. Oreo chased after him, trying to catch Aspen's flapping scarf. The cold rush of air against his face made him feel alive and excited. His heart pounding, he braced for the speed bump at the bottom of the hill and another wipeout in the powdery snow. After climbing back to the top of the hill, Aspen took a few minutes to crumble more snow pom-poms that collected on Oreo's fur before giving her a short ride down the hill.

After lunch they returned to the knoll and played several hours, too engrossed to notice that the sun was slipping behind the snow-covered mountain peaks, or that the lights surrounding the town square in the village had begun to illuminate. The new snow blanketing the valley resembled one of those tranquil postcards for sale at Buttrick's Bookstore.

It was after his last tumble at the bottom of the hill that Aspen noticed Oreo had not chased after him as she always did.

"Oreo! Oreo! Where are you?" he called. He heard Oreo's barking through the pine trees and caught a glimpse of her before vanishing deeper into the forest.

"Oh no, there she goes again," he said aloud and began to follow her paw prints in the snow.

They are so small, he thought, and then he noticed the deer tracks overlaying hers. Oreo was being followed!

Aspen's oversized winter boots made it difficult to move quickly through the snow, but he eventually made his way to the top of a small hill. From there, he could see Oreo in the distance, barking up at the treetops. He noticed a fat, old, gray squirrel scurrying from tree to tree. Its cheeks were stuffed with acorns that it collected during the warm days of autumn. Spotting the fat belly and the three white marks on her fur just under her chin, Aspen knew it was Pearl, one of Annie's favorite visitors to her birdfeeders. Pearl spent a fair amount of time stealing sunflower seeds whenever Scruff wasn't around, not that old fat Scruff could catch her anyway.

"Oreo," Aspen called out. "Oreo, Oreo."

Not hearing his call, Oreo chased Pearl, darting from tree to tree, further into the forest. Oreo was light enough to stay on top of the crusty snow, but Aspen's weight crumbled the crust below his feet and caused him to stumble, his boots filling with cold snow.

Aspen, now exhausted, caught up to her and twirled around before dropping backward into the snow. Oreo, covered in more snow, jumped on his chest and licked him on the face. Pearl now safe in her squirrel's nest high up in the trees with her trove of treasures, poked her nose out inquisitively as she watched the two of them. Aspen lay there, looking up at the sky, wishing on the first twinkling star he saw. It was then that he realized it was later than he thought, and that he was far from home, further in the woods than he had ever been before. He remembered the many hikes he took with his father and his father's best friend, Raulf Ludwig, on the Wapack Trails that wound through the forest between Bell Mountain Village and their mountaintop home.

Raulf helped build canoes in Topher's canoe shop, playfully named the Wooden Paddle. It is located half way up the gravel driveway, between the main road and the Pepin's home. Raulf is the candle maker, who owns and operates Wicks 'N Things Candle Shop across the town square from the Donut Fryer Bakery.

Topher and Raulf, like little boys, often came up with silly excuses to close up the canoe shop early in order to go hiking or fishing, and they took Aspen along whenever they could. "We need to go into town to get supplies," was the number one excuse given to Annie, but she always knew what they really were up to. Most supplies needed for the canoe shop were delivered 99 percent of the time. *Once a kid, always a kid,* Annie thought.

Many people came to hear Raulf spin his tales of growing up in the North Woods, hunting grizzly bears, but everyone knew there really weren't any grizzlies in New Hampshire and that Raulf was really a beaver trapper before becoming a candle maker.

As Aspen lie in the snow looking up at the treetops, the once familiar forest now seemed unfamiliar. He remembered passing the remnants of the old aluminum Christmas tree that someone stuck in the stone wall that ran along the embankment of a creek, and the remains of the old model-T Ford with young birch trees growing up through the rusted-out floor boards. An uneasy sensation began to stir inside of him. The light of the full moon reflected off the snow, and the dancing shadows of swaying trees spooked him.

Oreo tilted her head from side to side, watching Aspen with interest, wondering why he was lying in the snow, when a bird's chirp sounded in the distance, and off she ran.

"Oreo, Oreo," Aspen called out. *Why is she ignoring my calls to her? It's like she is making me follow her,* he thought. Aspen jumped to his feet and chased after his little friend. She finally came to a clearing near the top of a hill and sat down in the very center, waiting for him to catch up to her.

Aspen realized he was in a place he didn't recognize. "Oreo, what am I going to do with you? It's getting late, and we have to get home, you silly little dog."

As he turned to retrace his steps in the snow, Aspen's eyes opened wide in horror. In the dim light of the moon, the snow had its own story to tell. His trail of footprints crisscrossed in the snow. He was unable to tell from which direction he had come, or which way to go.

He held his hands against his numb ears as a chill danced across his skin. "I'm lost Oreo."

Lost in the Night

Aspen thought of his family, and he hoped they wouldn't worry about him since they knew he was in the Wapack Mountains and not some far off land. He knew the village was downhill from his mountaintop home, but he couldn't get his bearings. He found himself becoming frustrated and at the same time mesmerized by the show of lights the forest was putting on for him. Moonlight reflected off the icicles hanging from tree branches. Millions of ice crystals sparkled like diamonds in the snow. The forest wind softly whispered through the trees calling, "Assssspen."

It was getting cold, frostbite cold. Aspen knew he was lost and wouldn't be able to find his way home until daylight. He was afraid, and he didn't want Oreo to know it; he had to be a brave scout. It was up to him to protect her.

Aspen was a member of the Cub Scouts. He attended several hiking and camping trips with Mr. Quill, his scoutmaster. He had long, spiky, porcupine-like hair on the top of his head, something like a Mohawk. He also stuttered with any word that started with the letter *P*, causing his head to shake and his spikes of hair to quiver. Mr. Quill never took the laughter of the Scouts personally, in fact he often laughed at himself. Aspen was never sure if Mr. Quill was his real name or just a nickname that he grew accustomed to.

Mr. Quill often said to his pack of young boys, "If you ever got lost in the forest, stay where you are until someone finds you. Find nearby shelter and if p-p-possible build a fire to stay warm and dry, and most important of all, if you ever get lost in the winter, never fall asleep. You may not wake up."

Unfortunately, thanks to Oreo, this hike was unplanned, and Aspen didn't have the skills to build a campfire. He was still working toward his survival merit badge. He did remember that finding shelter was the most important thing to do. He decided that a lean-to would be the easiest to build, just like the one the scout group built during last summer's camping trip to Vermont. However, it was now dark and he could only see by the light of the moon. There was no time to build anything. Aspen wiped the single tear that ran down his cheek as he stood silently in the near darkness.

Aspen felt Oreo pushing against his leg. Looking down he saw that she was wet and shivering. He picked up his furry friend and tucked her into his warm red jacket. Her little nose stuck out like a baby kangaroo looking out of its mother's pouch.

From the center of the clearing, Aspen looked into the darkness of the tree line. His heart was pounding. His eyes scanned the horizon and made out the silhouette of a large pine tree, which could offer some protection from wind. Stepping in its direction, he heard a snapping beneath the tree. He squinted, struggling to see what might be there, but only darkness greeted him. He felt Oreo move inside his jacket.

"You're not afraid, are you?" he asked and gave her a kiss on her head. "Then neither am I."

He took another step forward. Snap, another branch broke, but the sound was moving away from the tree. He took a deep breath and cautiously walked toward the dark.

Reaching the tree, Aspen rested his back against the rough bark; the enormous girth of the trunk gave him a sense of security. He looked out into the darkness, and was struck by the feeling he was being watched, that he was not alone. He shook his head, trying to disregard the unpleasant thought.

A single gust of cold air howled through the trees calling, "Assssspen," and then the silence of the forest took over. Aspen squeezed Oreo a little tighter. He didn't notice the silhouette of Guardian, the moose from Contoocook Frog Pond, standing on a nearby crest, nor did he see the deer that had been keeping a watchful eye on him, the same deer that followed him as he wandered through the forest.

Ghostly shadows of the trees faded as clouds covered the moon. Aspen thought of the bedtime poem that Annie often recited to him when the north winds rattled his bedroom window on those cold winter nights: "Twinkling stars at night give way to snowflake flights ..."

"It's so quiet," Aspen whispered. He breathed softly, listening to the snowflakes landing on the tree branches next to his face. He gently gave Oreo another affectionate squeeze, and then wiped away the tears running down his cheeks.

"We'll be okay," he whispered in Oreo's ear as he recited, "Twinkling stars at night give way to snowflake flights, by this time tomorrow, all things will be shinny and bright, all back together from wrong to right ..."

Aspen struggled to keep his eyes open, but he couldn't; he was falling asleep, the one thing he didn't want to do, the one thing Mr. Quill said he shouldn't do.

The Sleigh Bell

Oreo poked her head out from Aspen's warm jacket when she heard the distinct sounds of "ch'ing, ch'ing, ch'ing" coming closer. A wooden sleigh approached the pine tree where Aspen lie sleeping; it creaked as it came to a stop. Oreo's tail thumped against Aspen's chest when she recognized the man standing on the back of the narrow, gray blue sleigh, and the single reindeer that pulled it.

She watched the man, in his long, brown, suede coat, step off the back of the sleigh. She let out a very soft bark, letting him know that she was glad to see him again. Careful not to wake Aspen, she climbed out of his jacket and ran into the arms of the man.

"So, your new name is Oreo now; it fits you well," he said with a hearty laugh as she licked his face.

The arched front of the sleigh was illuminated by a candle-lit copper lantern that hung beneath it. The man lifted the lantern off the wrought iron hook that held it in place. Stepping back, he held it next to the side of the sleigh.

The sound of the reindeer scratching at the snow with its hooves aroused Aspen. His eyes opened just enough to become aware of his surroundings. Unsure if he was awake or dreaming, he struggled to comprehend the oddly colored sleigh, and the person who was holding *his* Oreo. He was too exhausted, cold, and numb to speak; he could only watch.

The sleigh, although not much larger than the reindeer, was beautifully decorated with intricate, painted scrollwork resembling tarnished silver. A few less than a dozen or so sleigh bells were attached to the side of it, reflecting the soft yellow glow from the lantern. They were not like sleigh bells found in department stores, made of shiny gold or silver, and tied with red velvet ribbon; they were pewter gray, heavy, and thick. It was obvious they were a work of art. Each bell was handmade, a unique interpretation of an inspired thought. Some were decorated with markings of holly leaves, snowflakes, acorns, and pinecones; some with images of dwellings nestled in scenic mountains or deep forests. They were strung with a thin piece of leather and securely attached to small wrought iron hooks.

Aspen's gaze drifted from the stranger, to the bells, and then to the reindeer. It all seemed familiar somehow. As the man walked closer to the bells, they began to vibrate; each one sounding with its own distinctive tone, commanding his attention. However, one bell was louder than the others, vibrating so fast that it appeared to be singing.

"Aren't you the merrymaker?" the stranger said, and then chuckled out loud, his laughter echoing through the forest. "This must be yours Aspen."

Aspen could feel himself drifting, fighting to stay awake. The stranger gently lowered Oreo to the ground and he took off his dark leather mittens, sticking them into the pockets of his coat.

He then lifted the strap off the small wrought iron hook that held the sleigh bell in place. Unlike the others, this one had no markings on it; it was blank like a primed canvas waiting to be touched by the paintbrush of an artist. He walked toward Aspen and knelt down beside him, setting the lantern in the snow. The soft glow reflected on Aspen's pale, cold face as the stranger leaned close to Aspen's ear, and whispered, "Aspen, do you want to come home now?"

"Yes," was his answer. For a moment, Aspen felt he should go with this stranger, but then he sensed the man was not talking about his mountain home near Bell Mountain Village.

Aspen looked at Oreo, who stood next to the stranger. "No," he recanted. "I must get Oreo home, and I am lost."

The man smiled, pleased with Aspen's answer, pleased that he put Oreo's needs first.

"You are not lost, Aspen; you are only finding your way."

Aspen was not sure what was meant by this; he was just too cold and too tired to figure it out.

"I can't help you out of here, Aspen, but I will help you to help yourself. Just think about what you want most right now, and then think of how you will feel when you achieve it.

"Close your eyes for a moment and try to make a picture in your mind from the words that I will tell you. Imagine seeing yourself playing with Oreo in front of the warm fireplace in your living room. Smell the aroma of hot chocolate that your mother is stirring in the kitchen. There, your mother is filling mugs for you and your father. See your father flipping through the pages of his new backpacking magazine while sitting in his favorite chair. Can you smell the pine scent of the Christmas tree that you and your parents cut down at Fifield's Tree Farm?"

Aspen inhaled deeply the fragrance of the pine trees around him before drifting back to sleep.

"Sweet dreams," the man whispered to Aspen, who now lie quietly. The man's eyes teared; his heart filled with joy and love for Aspen. He speculated about the obstacles Aspen would have to overcome in his future, such as the darkness he encountered tonight. A wonderful life and a remarkable journey of self-awareness awaited this little boy. The man softly caressed Aspen's wet hair. He summoned the blue hare that was watching nearby and placed it upon Aspen's head to keep him warm.

"It's time for me to go," the stranger said to Oreo. He picked her up, giving her a generous hug as she once again licked his face. He laughed heartily, and then carefully opened Aspen's jacket, placed Oreo inside, and zipped it up to just under her chin, her head sticking out. The stranger reached into the small velvet bag hanging from the side of his boot, pulled out a star shaped biscuit, and he held it in front of Oreo's nose. She took the gift into her mouth then dropped it inside of Aspen's jacket.

"For such a little dog, you have a big heart and are truly dedicated, aren't you?"

Aspen stirred, struggling to open his heavy eyelids, and briefly glimpsed the man's outstretched hands that held the sleigh bell hanging from a leather strip. The stranger placed the sleigh bell around Aspen's neck.

The man picked up the lantern and returned to the back of the sleigh, where he reached into a compartment and pulled out a small, brown leather pouch bulging with round objects. He opened the drawstring and reached into the pouch, pulling out a new sleigh bell, and then placed the pouch back in the compartment. He walked over to where Aspen's sleigh bell had previously hung and filled the empty spot.

The new bell immediately began to vibrate. The stranger attached the lantern back on its wrought iron hook, and then turned to look where Aspen lay to make sure everything was just right. He stepped onto the floorboard of the sleigh, adjusted his footing, and grabbed the reins.

"I'll be seeing you soon, Oreo," he said, laughing aloud. "Tut, tut," he commanded, and the reindeer, laced in black leather harnesses, leaned forward taking up the slack in the reins.

"Tut, tut," he said again, and the sleigh creaked and lunged forward. Somewhere in the darkness of the woods, the last "ch'ing-ch'ing" faded into silence.

Oreo pulled her head inside Aspen's warm jacket, listened to the rhythm of Aspen's breathing, and fell asleep.

Finding Aspen

Earlier that evening, volunteers helped the Pepins search for Aspen. They were huddled around the blazing bonfire on the knoll, absorbing the heat it offered while sharing different ideas as to Aspen's disappearance. Their hope was that Aspen might see the glow of the fire and make his way home.

They made several attempts to find Aspen and Oreo. Flashlights proved to be of little use penetrating the curtain of falling snow into the darkness. All they could do was to wait for daybreak.

As morning approached, in the warmth of her kitchen, Annie cried softly to herself. She stirred the batch of bubbling hot chocolate and put up fresh coffee to perk on the old cast iron stove. It was the least she could do for the men and women who were enduring the cold night air. Scruff rubbed himself against Annie's leg, sensing that something was not right. Even Cluck, the rooster, was pacing in and out of the henhouse; he also sensed something was wrong.

Julie and Tanya Branhouser, Annie's best friends, were heating up bagels and muffins in Annie's oven. The sisters owned and operated the Donut Fryer Bakery next door to Wicks 'N Things Candle Shop. Julie was always a charming delight, a breath of fresh air, upbeat, happy and eager to great her customers. She giggled after almost every sentence she spoke. From under her worn-out baseball hat, her long auburn hair flipped into one big curl.

Tanya, on the other hand, could be prickly, like a thorn hiding on the stem of a beautiful yellow rose. Her blonde hair, pulled up tightly into a flawless bun that rested on top of her head, was held in place with a pink crochet hook. Customers that knew Tanya often challenged her rough exterior with a bear hug or a kiss on the cheek. She fussed and protested, "Get away from me," all the while blushing, trying to hide the twinkle in her eyes but never stepping away.

Overall, they were the two most kindhearted people you could meet. They truly enjoyed their customers, and they were very determined to make sure all felt welcome. A smile on their customers' faces meant more to them than the ringing of the old cash register.

"Don't ya worry, Annie," Tanya said in her New England accent, handing her a tissue to dry her tears.

"They will find Aspen," Julie finished Tanya's sentence with a giggle.

Outside Topher was sipping his coffee, feeling the warmth of the liquid settling in his stomach. A feeling of guilt overcame him as he stood next to the bonfire, wondering if Aspen was cold. He swallowed the last mouthful, twisted the cup back onto the top of the thermos, and placed it in the snow. *Aspen will be warm tomorrow, when he's home unwrapping his presents*, he thought.

"Did you hear that, Topher?" Raulf said excitedly.

Topher was standing with his hands chest high, fingertips touching, and palms spread apart. His head was slightly tilted, as if he was listening to something, but he didn't reply.

"Topher?" Raulf said softly, placing a hand on his friend's shoulder. "Topher?" he said even more softly this time, shaking his shoulder gently.

Raulf had the greatest respect for his friend, but he didn't always understand some of Topher's unusual ways. Raulf thought about the first time they met. When they were just boys, Topher pulled Raulf to safety after he had fallen through thin ice and into the freezing water of Whippoorwill Lake. They had been best of friends ever since.

"Yes, Raulf," Topher finally replied with a warm smile.

"I thought I heard bells," Raulf said looking up into the mountains.

"Ah, it must be the wind," he said shrugging his shoulders, not wanting Topher to think he was crazy.

"I thought I heard something as well, Raulf. In fact I'm sure I did, but I'm not exactly sure what I heard, or where it came from. Maybe it was music; maybe it was bells."

In silence, they looked toward the mountain range, both remembering bits and pieces of an old legend: the Legend of Bell Mountain. Were these the same kind of sounds people spoke about when the legend started? They both pondered the idea if the sounds they heard were somehow now connected to Aspen.

At the forest's edge, Topher, Raulf, and the search party waited for the ringing of the church bell that would announce dawn was close and they could soon begin their search in the forest.

Joey Bailey, the town mechanic, had a twenty-minute head start on his snowmobile. On the hillside, the lights from the machine disappeared into the trees, and the hum of the engine faded into silence.

As a young boy, Joey tinkered with any engine he could get his hands on, be it an old chain saw or seized-up lawn mowers he found at the local dump. When the opportunity presented itself to buy the abandoned garage on Howell Street, he purchased it, naming it the Town Mechanic, a reflection of his sense of humor. People loved him for it. He often pumped gas for his customers in costumes; in the fall he would dress as a scarecrow, at Easter he dressed as a bunny, and at Christmas he was an elf.

Topher suggested to Sheriff Carmichael that they head in the direction of Fiddler's Notch.

Sheriff Carmichael was what some people might call unique, six feet tall and lanky with red hair. When not on duty, he could be found in Buttrick's Bookstore reading up on quantum physics. His worn-out, pointed, black leather shoes, three sizes too big, were trimmed with gold buckles. His knee-high black socks were gathered at his ankles, contrasting with his skinny, hairless, pale, white legs. When not on duty, he wore black gym shorts, winter or summer, that hardly showed from under his oversized gray sweatshirt.

Despite his questionable fashion, he was liked very well, even adored. Extremely kindhearted and generous, he was always willing to help someone in need or volunteer for any worthwhile cause. People tried to avoid Sheriff Carmichael at times if he was seen walking around the village with a kitten in his hand or a puppy on a leash, knowing he was searching for an adoptive parent. He knew how to play the game well by putting fake diamond-studded collars on kittens and rainbow scarves around the necks of puppies. In all his years of being sheriff, he never brought a single stray to Windblown Animal Shelter; he found a home for every one of them.

"Why go in that direction?" Sheriff Carmichael asked.

"Fiddler's Notch is a well-known spot for hiking enthusiasts, even in winter," Raulf answered.

The view from Fiddler's Notch of the mountain range and the small Bell Mountain Village nestled within was Arcadian, postcard perfect. Even the most inexperienced hiker could climb to the notch in one afternoon. Fiddle players hiked up there several times a week to play their fiddles; they enjoyed the acoustics of the valley. Recreational hikers went up there nearly every day, summer or winter.

"If someone is there now, they might have seen Aspen," Topher added.

Topher and Raulf looked at each other. They both knew that they picked that particular direction because of the sounds they had heard the night before.

Sheriff Carmichael, Raulf, Topher, and a few other volunteers hiked up the East Ridge trail that intersected with the North Slope. The emerging morning view of the valley below was stunning. A few lanterns still twinkled softly in the sleepy village. Smoke from chimney tops drifted slowly away on unseen currents of air. Topher's heart swelled with gratitude for what his eyes beheld. He loved this place he called home. "Thank you," he whispered, giving thanks for what he had, an affirmation he made several times a day.

By the time the last shimmering star faded from the sky and the fingers of dawn crept in, the search party was deep into the forest. In the distance, they could hear the moan of Joey's snowmobile heading down Fisherman's Trail toward the village. The names of Aspen and Oreo echoed through the forest as volunteers called out for the missing pair.

Raulf and Topher turned onto an almost unnoticeable side trail. It led to a clearing near Fiddler's Notch, an area very special to Annie and Topher. Topher and Raulf froze in their tracks when they heard the faint, unmistakable sound of a jingling bell. Topher raised his finger to his lips signaling to Raulf to stay quiet. Again they heard the sound. Through deep snow, thickets, and laurel bushes, they ran toward the sound.

A trickle of blood ran down Topher's forehead where a stiff limb raked his face as he pushed through a thick grouping of hemlock. Stopping for a moment, they waited to hear the sound again, judging its direction.

They pursued the sound until they reached the edge of a small clearing. There they spotted a little black-and-white dog playing with a Mountain blue hare. It was Oreo. They watched as she chased the hare to one side of the clearing touching it, and then reversed her direction to let the hare chase after her. It was a funny sight.

Raulf and Topher looked at each other in bewilderment as the scene unfolded in front of them. On the opposite side of the clearing, just out of view, deer watched vigilantly. Topher noticed the snow in the clearing was imprinted with deer, moose, and smaller animal tracks; there were hundreds of tracks everywhere. The bare limbs of the hardwood trees and snow-covered branches of the pine trees surrounding the clearing were alive with sounds and movements of birds. White-throated sparrows, blue jays, chickadees, yellow grosbeaks, buntings, and finches all darted about. Even the elusive rain crow made an appearance.

Raulf and Topher stood motionless watching the scene until the sound of a bell reclaimed their attention. It was then, that they saw the sleigh bell around Oreo's neck for the first time.

"Oreo," Topher called out.

Oreo and the hare stopped their game and turned to see where the voice came from. Oreo's tail began to wag as she recognized the familiar faces of Raulf and Topher. She gave the hare a lick on its furry face to indicate the game was over. The hare twitched its nose, bounced over to where the two deer stood, and then turned back to look at Oreo as if to say good-bye. Oreo bounced through the snow, her bushy tail wagging and her ears flopping. With one big leap she jumped into Topher's arms and licked his prickly unshaven face.

"Oreo, where is Aspen? Can you find Aspen?" Topher said.

Oreo began to wiggle and squirm in his arms. He set her down, and she ran to the opposite side of the clearing where an unusually large pine tree had grown. There, at the base of the tree, Topher could see something red. It was Aspen's jacket.

Topher and Raulf called out Aspen's name, but he didn't move. Fear that Aspen could be dead, raced through Topher. "Aspen," they called out as they ran toward the motionless body lying under the tree. They had to crouch down to get under the pine boughs heavily laden with snow.

"Aspen," Topher said softly, cupping Aspen's face in the palms of his hands. "He's okay! He's incoherent but okay!"

Topher reached down to lift Aspen when, he noticed two large impressions of melted snow on either side of his boy. Topher glanced up the hill just in time to see two white tailed deer and the blue hare disappear over a small knoll into the forest. He never noticed the silhouette of Guardian, who stood at the wayside. Satisfied that Aspen was safe, the moose disappeared into the forest; for now its job was complete.

Topher gently lifted Aspen into his arms, noticing he was much warmer than he should have been after being in the woods overnight without any protection.

Raulf saw the star-shaped biscuit fall from Aspen's jacket as Topher lifted him up into his arms. He picked up the biscuit, examined the unusual shape, and turned toward little Oreo.

"This must be yours," Raulf said. He placed the biscuit in his pocket, picked her up, and followed Topher down the mountainside.

The church bells tolled in Bell Mountain Village announcing the good news, spreading word of Aspen's rescue. The first settlers of the village had decided the church bells were to ring for only two reasons: to announce the time of day and to announce good news. To this day the practice is still used.

Christmas Morning

Julie and Tanya Branhouser left the Pepin home early that morning to open the Donut Fryer Bakery. The aroma of coffee beans tumbling in the vintage cast iron roaster and fresh-baked pastries drifted down the sidewalks of the village square. It was Christmas Day and Christmas Jubilee would be starting soon. This was one of the busiest weeks of the year for the Branhouser sisters, and with the latest news of Aspen's safe return, it was sure to be an exciting and profitable day.

During the celebration, the streets around the town square were restricted to horse-drawn sleighs and foot traffic. The Adirondack gazebo was divided into two sections: one side was for the selling of hot apple cider and hot chocolate, and the other side was reserved for the oompah band which would be arriving at noon. Christmas music softly played through speakers that temporarily hung from the gas-lit street lanterns lining the square. Carolers in European-style costumes leisurely walked around the village visiting shop owners and talking to people in the square, promoting that night's performance of *A Christmas Carol* at Hastings Playhouse.

Julie and Tanya knew that Irene and Bill Quantock would be the first customers to arrive at their bakery. Two hot chocolates and warm cinnamon rolls dripping with white icing would be ready for them, along with a bag of day-old bread. After leaving the bakery, Bill and Irene would stroll over to the far end of the town square where there was a large water fountain surrounded by park benches. The fountain was drained during the winter and used as an oversized bird feeder until spring when the water would be turned back on. At the fountain, they would break apart the old bread and feed it to the yellow grosbeaks, chickadees, pigeons, and any other birds that migrated their way. "God's little creatures," Irene would call them.

Back at the Pepin home, Annie could not hear the tolling of the church bell through the stone walls of her home and didn't know Aspen had been found. Scruff watched in silence as Annie placed the last of the presents under the Christmas tree. Wonderful memories filled her heart as she looked at the old collection of ornaments that hung on the tree. She gently touched the hundred-plus-year-old hollow egg painted with a scene of a horse-drawn sleigh and a red covered bridge. The delicate ornament had been handed down through several generations on Topher's side of the family. Topher wasn't exactly sure when it was made or by whom. The painting was signed with a small star and dated eighteen hundred and … the rest of the date was faded and unreadable.

Annie's thoughts traveled into the past as she observed each ornament, her eyes coming to rest on the small picture framed in birch bark. It contained a picture of Aspen celebrating Christmas. She was filled with emotion as she thought of the day Aspen presented it to her after coming home from summer camp. He was so proud of it. Her eyes teared as she fondled the small frame and visualized his infectious smile. She wondered if perhaps he was gone forever.

Annie closed her eyes envisioning that Christmas Eve night when she and Topher were winter camping up near Fiddler's Notch. Weather permitting, they preferred to sleep outside of their tent, under the night sky, snuggled in warm sleeping bags. That night they scanned the Milky Way, admiring the twinkling stars against the dark sky and debating whether they evolved on their own or whether a magnificent power just wished them into existence. A shooting star etched a path through the night sky; Annie silently wished upon it for a child to call her own. Unbeknownst to her, Topher was wishing for the same thing.

"Shhh, Topher, listen to the church bells echoing in the valley. Aren't they lovely?" Annie asked.

"I hear them, Annie, but they aren't coming from below; they are coming from the forest. Maybe it's the bell maker, you know the man people talk about in the Bell Mountain Legend," he said teasingly.

That Christmas morning was beautiful, crisp, and clear. That's when they heard the laughter of a child and followed it until they found a little boy playing with a rabbit under the barren branches of an aspen tree. They guessed he was about four years old. He couldn't remember his name, where he came from, or how he got there.

They took him home and cared for him, and when no one came for him, they started the process to legally adopt him. Their wish had come true.

They named him Aspen, after the tree under which he was found. They felt he was like that tree, dormant and ready to grow, and one day he would come to know his true self, his true origins. Annie knew that someday that mystery would be solved, but the last thing she wanted, was for Aspen to leave as mysteriously as he had come. She and Topher both loved Aspen so very much.

"Not yet!" she yelled out loud, wakening herself from her daydream. She deeply inhaled the scent of Christmas and regained her composure.

Scruff saw Annie heading toward him and stiffened. She grabbed him up off the couch and scratched his head nervously while walking over to the frosted window that overlooked the yard and driveway. The snow was plowed high against the split-rail fence. Only the tops with their decorations of plastic red Christmas bows poked through.

Annie was absentmindedly rocking Scruff like a baby when her eyes caught movement. It was Topher's beautiful, old pickup truck coming up the driveway. Behind him was Sheriff Carmichael and some of the other members of the search team. Horns were honking, lights were flashing, and people were cheering out their windows.

Scruff found himself being hurdled through the air toward the couch as Annie ran to the front door and flung it wide open. Tears of joy ran down her face as she saw Aspen's red jacket through the windshield of Topher's truck.

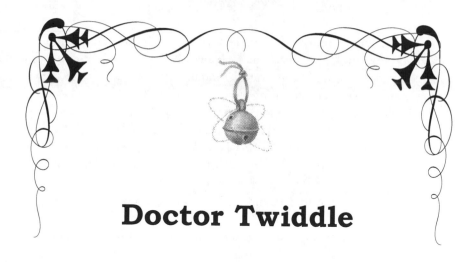

Doctor Twiddle

It was 10:00 am on Christmas morning, and Aspen lay sleeping with Oreo cuddled next to him. Dr. Twiddle quietly closed Aspen's bedroom door behind him and went into the kitchen.

Topher poured a cup of coffee for the doctor as he sat down at the kitchen table.

"Other than being hungry, tired, and a little cold, Aspen is just fine, as is his little dog," Dr. Twiddle explained.

Annie, now seated beside Topher, sighed with relief.

"It's a Christmas miracle that he didn't die of exposha," Dr. Twiddle said with his Down East accent. "The temperacha was frost-biting cold last night, but Aspen had not even the slightest sign of frostbite. In fact," Dr. Twiddle unconsciously twisting his handlebar mustache said, "he's no worse for the wear. He is in remarkable condition for sure, and I bet he will be up and ready to open his Christmas presents shortly. Mr. Pepin, do ya have any idea what led Aspen up to the woods last night? What he might have been doing?"

Topher explained how his son had been sledding on the knoll as he did frequently. "But when we called him in for supper, he was nowhere to be found."

"Nor was Oreo," Annie added. "We knew something was wrong and that they must have wandered off."

"Did anything unusual happen here yesterday afternoon or evening that you can think of?" asked Dr. Twiddle.

"Just the sounds coming from the mountains." Topher realized he now would have to explain himself.

Topher continued. "While Raulf and I waited with the others on the knoll, we heard beautiful, soft sounds, like bells, echoing down the valley from the area of Fiddler's Notch. Not church bells, but the kind that you would jingle." Topher motioned with his hand, back and forth.

Dr. Twiddle, not understanding, frowned and scratched the side of his forehead.

"It was the sound of a bell that was placed around Oreo's neck that led us to her, and she led us to Aspen."

Dr. Twiddle leaned toward Topher and looked him directly in the eye. "Is there anything else, Mr. Pepin?"

"Well," Topher began, pausing to formulate the right words. "There were the animals."

"The animals, of course." Dr. Twiddle's eyes twinkled as he again twisted the end of his mustache.

Topher explained how he and Raulf saw hundreds of animal tracks in the snow. "There were deer tracks where Aspen had lain sleeping and two melted areas of snow exposing the grass where deer apparently slept next to him, keeping him warm through the night."

Topher and Raulf were unaware that Guardian had also kept close watch over him.

Annie looked at Topher. She could tell by his wrinkled forehead that he was struggling, trying to explain the events without sounding like a bubblehead. She smiled warmly, squeezing his hand, and nodded in approval for him to continue.

"There were other tracks in the snow as well."

"Oh?" Dr. Twiddle motioned with his hand to continue.

"There were sleigh tracks in the snow—I think they were sleigh tracks," he quickly added as if to defend his sanity. "And there was a single set of footprints leading over to where Aspen had lain, sleeping under the large pine tree where we found him."

"Do you know whose footprints they were? Do you have any idea where the sleigh tracks came from?"

"The answer is no to both questions."

The prodding Dr. Twiddle asked, "What prompted you to tie such a big sleigh bell on such a little dog?"

Topher wondered how Dr. Twiddle knew the bell was in fact too big for a little dog or that the bell was actually a sleigh bell. Neither he nor Annie had mentioned either of these facts. Topher was about to ask the doctor when Annie's fidgeting interrupted his thoughts.

Annie looked toward Aspen's room as she answered the doctor's last question. "We have never seen that bell before." Annie stood up and walked over to the fireplace mantel, giving Scruff a quick pat on his head as she passed by the couch where he lay. She brought the sleigh bell back to the table and handed it to Dr. Twiddle. He could hardly conceal his excitement while examining it.

"Why, that looks like a sleigh bell, a very old sleigh bell for sure," he said. He raised his eyebrows as if he had no idea what kind of bell it was.

He seemed to be looking for something in particular as he turned the sleigh bell over in his hands. "Can't say I ever saw such a bell like this. It's different," he mumbled to himself.

Topher surmised that Dr. Twiddle had indeed seen something like this before. "What do you mean different? In what way?" Topher asked.

"Oh, what I mean is that it must have taken someone a long time to make. Look at the tiny marks made by the metal being hammered into its round shape. Strange though," he added, twirling the bell in one hand while fiddling with the end of his mustache with the other. "It looks like it's made in one piece, with no seam, yet somehow the small metal pellet is inside." He glanced up to see if he had their attention.

Topher caught the questioning glance of the doctor. Was he asking or actually explaining how the bell was made? Topher also noticed the twinkle in the doctor's eyes and a faint grin on his face. Was he looking at something familiar? *Yes, the doctor knows something*, Topher thought, and he was right.

This was not the first time Dr. Twiddle was called upon to examine someone who had had a similar encounter. He kept a very extensive scrapbook with photographs, drawings, and newspaper clippings of any event in the Wapack Valley that involved a sleigh bell or a mysterious stranger. However, none of his records had any references of the stranger leaving a sleigh bell with animals. Someone else must have put the sleigh bell on Oreo. The doctor was about to ask more questions when

Oreo ran into the kitchen and interrupted the conversation. Aspen appeared right behind her, barefooted and dressed in flannel pajamas decorated with deer, moose, and bear.

"Merry Christmas," Aspen yelled out as he gave each of them a hug. Dr. Twiddle graciously accepted his unexpected hug as well. Aspen was just that kind of boy, accepting everyone, acting as if he had known them all his life.

"How are you feeling this morning, you young whippersnappa?" the doctor asked.

"It's all good," Aspen replied with an enormous smile. He always used this phrase. It was one of the first sentences he had ever spoken, and the Pepins never did figure out where he had learned it.

Apparently, Aspen had no recollection of the events of the night before, and seeing that the boy was in good health and fine spirits, Dr. Twiddle concluded his visit. He stood up to leave and wished them all a Merry Christmas and a Happy New Year. Topher opened the arched wooden door, walked the doctor out into the yard, and helped brush off the few inches of snow that had accumulated on the car during his visit.

Topher reached to shake Dr. Twiddle's hand. "Thank you for coming all the way up here to examine Aspen, especially on Christmas morning."

Dr. Twiddle smiled, gave Topher a wink of an eye, and bid him farewell.

Back in the house, Annie asked Aspen if he would find a perfect spot on the Christmas tree for his new ornament.

"My ornament, where did it come from?" he asked as he placed the sleigh bell next to the small birch frame that held his picture.

"There's a story connected to the new ornament, sweetie." Annie was not sure how to explain the sleigh bell; she hoped he might remember something about it later. "It's Christmas morning, and we have presents to open!" Annie stated tickling Aspen in order to avoid the question.

That evening, as twilight fell and the first stars came out of hiding, the Pepins gathered on the knoll to view the twinkling lights of the village nestled in the valley below. The weeklong Christmas Jubilee was under way and the voices of the carolers singing around the lit Christmas tree in the town square echoed up the valley. Listening to the joyful sounds, they gave thanks for all the blessings in their lives and the blessings yet to come.

Mona Foresight,
the Reporter

The Donut Fryer Bakery opened early the day after Christmas, giving off the delicious smell of freshly baked pastries and brewed coffee. The regulars, including Bill and Irene Quantock, gathered early. The buzz of voices was louder than usual; everyone was eager to share their version of Aspen's rescue.

Julie hummed Christmas tunes as she poured steaming coffee for her guests. Even Tanya, who was normally very grumpy this time of morning, was in a festive mood.

The Quantocks had a very special reason to be the first in line that morning. Bill placed their usual order at the counter while Irene mumbled as she rearranged the tables and chairs to her liking. She made sure her chair faced the door so she could greet the people she knew entering the bakery, and size up the ones she didn't. She pretended that it was a bother to be so popular, but anyone could tell she enjoyed the morning gatherings and being the Donut Fryer's honoree hostess. The Quantocks just seemed to attract people who enjoyed their carefree personalities. Bill often sat in compatible silence as Irene picked the topic of the day and orchestrated the conversation.

"Irene and I want coffee to be on us for every customer today," Bill informed Julie and Tanya.

The sisters looked at each other and then looked back at Bill. Julie, who fancied Mr. Quantock, blushed. "Why do you want to do that, Bill—I mean Mr. Quantock?"

He explained it was their way to celebrate the good news of Aspen's rescue, and to give a holiday gift to the good folks of the village. "And don't keep it under your hat," he said, as he jokingly patted his bald head. "Tell every customer the coffee is free today."

With people chatting, coffee cups clanging, and the ringing of the old pushbutton cash register, no one noticed the stranger sitting in the corner. Her beehive style hairdo was decorated with plastic daisies awkwardly tilted to one side. Her eyes peeped over the top of her notebook, through horn-rimmed, pink, imitation diamond-studded eyeglasses.

She was Mona Foresight, the reporter from Peterborough's *Say What You Gata Say Gazetteer*. She was often at the bakery eavesdropping, looking for a new story to report. The news of the lost boy and his dog was not new, but Mona had an idea in mind. She could always smell a good story where no one else could.

"Ten-year-old lost in the treacherous Wapack Mountains on Christmas Eve"—the perfect headline, she thought. Mona was a great person to know and to have as a friend if you didn't mind her snooping into your business. She was quite jolly, warmhearted, generous, and fair about things except for one: his name was Lonnie, her rival, who was also a reporter for *Say What You Gata Say Gazetteer*. They were actually good friends now, and their friendship thrived on their competitiveness.

Mona could sense Lonnie was around somewhere, trying to use his witty charm to beat her to a story. She wasn't about to let that happen. Five minutes later, Mona and a box of freshly baked pastries were headed up the mountainside in her vintage 1967 VW bus painted with peace signs and big white daisies.

Annie, was out in the front yard filling bird feeders that hung from the barren branches of the old maple tree. She was startled by the loud backfire of the VW bus as it plowed through the two-foot snowbank at the end of the driveway. She immediately recognized the custom paintjob on the VW bus. She waved to Mona, motioning to follow her inside.

Mona sat at the kitchen table as Aspen doodled in his new sketchbook in front of the fireplace hearth. She placed the box of pastries on the table, offering Annie and Topher first pick, and began to explain the reason for her visit.

"By now, everyone in the valley has heard about Aspen's terrible night in the woods, being attacked by a wild man and rabid beasts of all kinds."

Annie and Topher looked at each other, stunned.

Mona laughed, grinning from ear to ear. "I'm only kidding," she said, "but that is the kind of story some people are spreading around. My intent is to document it correctly, with your permission of course. Aspen's adventure is remarkable, and it would be a great story to start out the New Year. It would give inspiration and hope to all that read it, letting them know that miracles do happen and that there are good people out in the world, even if their identity is unknown. It must be shared," Mona added emphatically.

Annie and Topher agreed. They began to explain how Aspen became lost in the woods looking for Oreo, how the search was delayed due to darkness, and how the sound of bells coming from the mountains could be heard during the night.

"The Legend of Bell Mountain?" Mona asked.

The Pepins looked at each other, unsure how to answer the question.

"Mr. Pepin, how did Aspen survive the cold night with only a jacket?" she asked, adjusting her crooked glasses.

"Apparently the animals kept him warm and safe," Topher said as he looked over toward Aspen. He was waiting for some sort of reaction from Mona but none came.

"Oh," she said without even looking up, and continued scribbling in her notebook. "How was Aspen eventually found?" she continued. There was no reply.

Mona raised her head just enough to look over the top of her notebook, her eyes shifting from Annie to Topher and back again.

"We heard the bell," Topher said, breaking the silence. "It was hanging around Oreo's neck."

"The bell?" Mona asked. "So it's true what everyone is saying?" she asked as she dipped her cinnamon bun into her cup of coffee.

Topher replied, "Yes, that is true. Raulf and I heard the sound of

Oreo's bell, which guided us to the place where she was playing with a rabbit."

"The blue hare," Mona said as she wrote in her notebook trying to hide the excitement building up inside of her.

Topher wondered how Mona knew the rabbit was in fact a blue hare. *It seems as though a few people around here know more than they are telling.*

"Oh, how smart of you to do that, put a bell on Oreo. I wish more people would do that for their pets. That would shorten the lost-and-found pet column," Mona said.

Again, there was no reply. "Is there more?" she asked. Mona absentmindedly fooled with the top of her beehive that was beginning to unravel.

Topher raised his hands in the air suggesting the unknown. "We don't know where the bell came from. We never saw it before. The first time was the morning Aspen was found."

"Oh," Mona said shifting in her seat. This story was getting better all the time. Mona squinted as she glanced out the front window, expecting to see her rival Lonnie coming up the driveway. "Where do you think it came from?"

"We don't know," said Annie. "I think it's time to ask Aspen himself. Don't you think so, honey?" She reached over and gently squeezed Topher's hand.

Topher looked lovingly at Annie and nodded in agreement.

Topher excused himself from the table and walked over to the stone fireplace where Aspen was playing. "There's someone here to ask you some questions about the other night," he said. He kneeled down beside Aspen and stroked his hair. "Do you mind?"

Aspen stood up and gave his father a big smile and hug. "Nope, I don't mind."

Mona sat open-mouthed as Aspen came over to her and wrapped his arms around her. "I'm Aspen, and this is my dog Oreo," he announced. "Who are you?"

"I'm Miss Foresight, sweetie, but you can call me Mona," she replied.

Aspen blushed. He didn't particularly like being called sweetie now that he was ten and almost a man.

"Your mother and father have been telling me about your terrifying night in the woods."

"Ah shucks, I wasn't afraid," he replied.

"Can you tell me about the sleigh bell that was found around Oreo's neck?" she asked.

Aspen ran over to the Christmas tree, took a bell off the pine bough, and ran back to the table. "This one," he shouted over the ringing as he swung it in circles over his head.

"Yes, I believe so," Mona replied, looking at Annie and Topher for acknowledgement.

"What do you want to know?" he asked.

"Where did you get it from, and did you put it on Oreo?"

"I gave her the bell when the deer came. I was afraid she would chase them, and I would have to go after her again. I was afraid she might get too far ahead of me."

"So you had the bell before you went into the woods?"

"No," Aspen replied, "the man gave it to me."

The three adults sat upright at this.

"The man, what man?" Annie asked.

A shiver ran down Topher's back as he recalled the footprints in the snow leading from the sleigh tracks over to where Aspen lay.

"The man with the funny-looking deer and the singing bells," said Aspen.

"Singing bells!" Mona repeated, staring at him through her coke-bottle glasses.

"They—," Aspen paused, trying to think of just the right words to say. "They just kind of sang." Aspen's face gleamed with pride. "And the one that sang the loudest, he gave to me! He put it around my neck when he thought I was sleeping."

"Oh, I see," said Mona. "Can you show us how it sings?"

Aspen shrugged his shoulders indicating he couldn't.

"What else do you remember son?" Topher asked.

"He asked me to think."

"Think about what?" Mona asked.

"To think about what things are the most important to me. That's when the two deer from the woods came to keep me warm."

Topher remembered how the animals had left in the same direction when he and Raulf approached Aspen that morning in the forest. He'd wondered where they were heading.

The legend, I knew it, Mona thought. *It has to be.*

"What else, sweetie?" Annie asked. "Do you remember anything else?"

"Nah, I guess I fell asleep," he answered. He looked down at Oreo, who was tugging at the leg of his pajama bottoms, her bushy tail wagging. "Can I go play now?"

"Sure, son," said Topher. He felt his son had answered enough questions for one day.

"Aspen, if it's okay with your mom and dad, may I ask you one more question, please?" said Mona.

Aspen shrugged his shoulders.

"Aspen, what was your answer when the man asked you what was important to you?"

"I don't remember," Aspen replied.

Mona knew he was holding back, avoiding the question, but for what reason?

"Why don't you and Oreo go play now?" Topher could see that his son was hesitating, not ready to share anything further at this time.

Aspen took the sleigh bell and placed it back on the tree. His palm tingled, and a strange sensation came over him. He sat on the floor staring at the sleigh bell. He picked up the sketchpad that Santa left him and began to draw a picture of a path leading into a beautiful pasture.

Mona glanced at the window again, and then gathered up her things and thanked Annie and Topher for their gracious hospitality. "Thank you for your help, Aspen," she said as she headed for the front door.

Without being prompted, Aspen jumped up, ran over to Mona, and gave her a hug as though they were bosom buddies.

Mona smiled. "I'll send you a copy of the article," she said, then closed the large wooden door behind her with a resounding click. The VW bus backfired and exhaled puffs of smoke as it headed back down the snow-covered driveway.

The story was published on New Year's Day in *Say What You Gata Say Gazetteer,* but the story didn't fade away after the first printing.

Aspen's story was reprinted many times during subsequent holiday seasons, and the Legend of Bell Mountain became a favorite holiday tale for many people. Letters addressed to Aspen began arriving after the story was initially printed. Some even came addressed to Oreo. The few letters that Annie and Topher did read captured their imaginations as each contained a story that some people would call a miracle.

Annie and Topher decided the rest of the letters should be unopened and given to Aspen when he was older. They belonged to him; only he could truly appreciate the stories that other people had offered to share with him. The letters kept arriving over the years, and as they did, Annie put them in a box with the others.

The sleigh bell found its permanent place on the fireplace mantel, hanging in a small, red velvet-lined shadow box. It was a constant reminder of how the world is full of wonder, and how valuable and great life can truly be.

Aspen Grows Up

Aspen had numerous hobbies growing up. One of his favorites was the making and playing of fiddles. This hobby paved the way to his becoming the best luthier in New Hampshire. By the age of twenty-two, he had also become a master canoe builder, just like his father. He had enjoyed the craft of woodworking as a young boy; it came naturally for him. Now as a young man, he felt lucky to continue his family tradition.

The rising of Little Moose River was the main factor for the Pepins to relocate the Wooden Paddle to the far end of the knoll. It was also an opportunity to upgrade the machinery. The rear of the new canoe shop had two large retractable doors that when opened overlooked the Wapack Mountain range. The view was inspiring. While working, Aspen and his father would often tune the radio to instrumental music. The music, combined with the view of the valley, made them feel as if they owned their own piece of paradise.

Often Annie would see the both of them standing in silence on the grass behind the shop, facing the valley. Their eyes were sometimes closed, sometimes opened; their hands were raised chest high and with fingers touching, their palms pushed apart as if they were holding something in between, and their faces were radiant, lit up by a faint smile.

Watching them, Annie could sense their mood of gratitude and fulfillment. However, she didn't understand the ritual between father and son, and she wasn't sure when they started this practice. She didn't know if the father was teaching the son or if the son was teaching the father. Perhaps they were taught the practice at the last Indian Pow-Wow at the Kidder Mountain Fair Grounds. She never interrupted them and never asked for an explanation. In her heart, she simply felt it was good, it was right; some things shared between a father and a son should be just for them, just as some things between a mother and a daughter should be.

Aspen loved the valley and all it had to offer. Except for the addition of Hastings's Playhouse, not much has changed over the years in Bell Mountain Village. The Sip-N-Dip coffee stand found a permanent home in the old train depot next to the Cider Mill at the far end of town. The parking expanded behind the coffee shop for snowmobile riders coming off the New Hampshire State Snowmobile Trail that ran from southern New Hampshire to the most northern town of Pittsburg. The expansion of the Kidder Mountain Fair Grounds, north of the village, included an outdoor amphitheater and a separate twenty-acre parcel for the annual Native American Music festival.

With the smell of autumn in the air and winter approaching, Aspen spent extra time preparing for the annual Christmas fundraiser that supported local charities. His favorite project was the building of the wooden canoe. It would be raffled off, and some of the proceeds would be donated to Windblown Animal Shelter. Aspen's heart soared with joy whenever he was helping the animals at the shelter, never forgetting this was where he first saw Oreo. Occasionally, he would contemplate about where Oreo might have lived before being adopted. Did someone abandon her, or did she just lose her way? Perhaps she just wanted to venture out into the world and struck out on her own.

Aspen loved autumn walks down the old dirt roads near his home. The palette of colors and the aroma of the countryside were intoxicating to his senses. He laughed as Oreo ran through piles of gold, brown, and red leaves.

"Where do you get your unyielding energy?" he called to her. "You're as rambunctious as the day we adopted you." He wondered how old she really was; she was always playful like a puppy and seemed never to age.

Aspen deeply inhaled the scent of the forest that was about to begin its long winter sleep. A faded memory of someone telling him to breathe in the scent of pine stirred within him, but he couldn't place the person. He tried to sneak up on Oreo, to give her bushy tail a little tug, a game they often played. The crunching of the dry leaves under his feet often warned her of his approach, giving her a chance to dart away. Scruff, older now, never followed beyond the end of the driveway. He couldn't be bothered with such silly things as nature walks. Nevertheless, he was always there, waiting for Aspen's return home.

The Awakening

Christmas was fast approaching, and it was time to make the annual quarter-mile trip to Fifield's Alpine Haus. Topher and Aspen pulled Annie on the old toboggan that was to be used to haul the spruce tree back home. Oreo sat in Annie's lap. "Mush, mush, faster, faster," Annie teased them.

Aspen went to look for the perfect tree while Annie and Topher shared hot apple cider in the gift shop. Folks came from as far away as Maine and Vermont to cut their own Christmas trees or to enjoy a day of cross-country skiing. Ski trails linked most of the valley together, and a fair amount of them led to the village square. During the winter months, wooden ski trees took the place of bicycle racks.

"Did you find a tree to cut?" asked Mr. Fifield.

"No, but Oreo did." Aspen laughed as he explained how Oreo kept barking at a tree in which an American three-toed woodpecker sang to its captive audience.

Mr. Fifield tied the spruce to the toboggan. He knelt down, gave Oreo a pat on the head, and tossed her a star-shaped biscuit. He never knew which of his customers it was that kept leaving treats on the stone hearth in the dining area of the restaurant. He kept a watchful eye on them, but he never found out who, or why, someone keep leaving the treats anonymously. Yet every couple of weeks he would find a small paper bag of biscuits, and the only clue as to who the giver might be was a star stamped on the side of the bag. Since Mr. Fifield was a foster parent to service dogs, he speculated that this might be someone's way of rewarding his kindness.

On the way home, Topher and Annie pulled the toboggan while Oreo took the coachman's role, her paws hanging over the rounded front. Aspen tagged along in the rear, intrigued by the two deer that seem to be following them through the forest.

"Jingle Bells, jingle bells, jingle all the way …," they sang on the way home, their voices joyful.

That night the Pepins popped popcorn the old fashioned way, in a wire screen over the open flames in the fireplace. Oreo and Scruff waited anxiously for stray kernels that dropped onto the floor. Christmas music played in the background as the Pepins hung ornaments and discussed who would be making the hot chocolate that they would be bringing to the tree-lighting ceremony in the village town square. When it came to loving the holiday season, the Pepins were like little children.

Aspen noticed his mother standing next to the fireplace with a smile on her face. She was looking at the last ornament that needed placing on the Christmas tree.

"Everything okay, Mom?" Aspen asked as he stood next to her, wrapping his arms around her shoulders and giving her a gentle squeeze.

"It's all good," she said. She laughed as she took the small wooden box containing the sleigh bell off the mantle and placed it in Aspen's hand. She looked into her son's eyes and saw something she had not noticed before. His eyes still sparkled whenever he smiled, but they were no longer the eyes of her small boy; now they were the eyes of a young man.

Annie felt the tightness in her stomach that parents often do when they realize their children have grown up in what seemed to be a blink of the eye. Aspen had become a young man, and she felt the time was getting close when he would journey into his past. Although he had never questioned his past, her motherly intuition told her he was at the very least thinking about it.

For the past twelve years, Aspen had been the one who placed the sleigh bell on the Christmas tree. This time, however, as the weight of the sleigh bell left his hand, he felt a slight tingle in his palm. He thought of the first time he placed the sleigh bell on the Christmas tree when he was just a boy, and he felt the same tingle. He slowly reached toward it, and again he felt the vibration.

"Are you ready?" Topher called out breaking Aspen's train of thought. Topher was waiting at the front door holding the thermoses filled with hot chocolate. He was eager to get to the town square before the lights on the Christmas tree were lit.

"For sure," Aspen said, stepping away from the sleigh bell. The sensation faded from his palm. Aspen placed the fireplace screen on the stone hearth, securing it to the wrought iron hooks that protruded from the stone facing. On his way out, he grabbed his coat and scarf off the hat rack next to the door. "You be a good girl!" he shouted to Oreo on his way out. "No chasing Scruff." He glanced one more time at the sleigh bell and headed toward the door.

Annie unplugged the electrical cords from the wall outlets that powered the lights on the Christmas tree. "And you be a good cat," she said to Scruff, and then she closed the door on her way out.

The twenty-five-foot spruce tree that Mr. Fifield donated to Bell Mountain Village was strung with old fashion lights: big bulbs of red, blue, yellow, and green. As eight o'clock approached, people drifted toward the town square. Bill and Irene Quantock helped Raulf pass out small white candles that he had made especially for this. At a quarter till eight, the Hasting House Carolers began their rendition of the "Twelve Days of Christmas," and the crowd lit their candles. At eight o'clock sharp, Joey Bailey pulled the cord to the generator; it started, giving power to the extension cords connected to the tree. Everyone clapped and whistled as the old bulbs came to life. The oompa band began to play while adults shared salutations and children lined up for a sleigh ride around the square.

Aspen was in high spirits, enjoying the festive events, when his attention was caught by a faint, familiar sound of something ringing. The flurry of events surrounding him faded into the background, and for a moment, time seemed to stand still. He turned to look up the valley in the direction where the sound was coming from. Unconsciously he put his hands together, as he had with his father so many times before.

"Aspen, my darling cupcake," Julie Branhouser called as she darted through the crowds extending her arms, aiming her hug.

"No, he's my cupcake," Tanya said, as she threw her arms around

Aspen from the opposite side. These were the first of many hugs given to him that night.

"Oh, Christmas tree, oh, Christmas tree, how shiny are your branches," Aspen sang along with the others. He was truly enjoying their fellowship, but a portion of his consciousness remained on the ringing sound and the sleigh bell that hung on their family Christmas tree.

That night Annie and Topher prepared themselves for bed while Aspen stoked the coals in the fireplace. He kept looking over at the Christmas tree.

Annie came in the living room to find the novel she had started reading the night before. "Deep in thought?" she asked, noticing Aspen was staring into the flickering flames.

Aspen smiled, stood up, and walked over to the Christmas tree. He reached into the tree and held the sleigh bell in his hand. "I thought I heard something earlier, at the tree lighting ceremony. I thought I heard bells."

"Oh, sweetie, a lot of people were walking around with and shaking Christmas bells. What's so unusual about that?"

"No ...," Aspen paused. "Up in the mountains, I heard the sounds coming from there."

Aspen didn't notice his mother flinch as a shiver danced on her skin.

The now familiar tingling in his palm lingered a little longer this time as he let go of the sleigh bell. He turned to give his mother a hug. "Never mind, you're right; it must have been the carolers' bells." It hurt him to be untruthful, but he felt this was not the time to venture into this unknown area.

Annie gave Aspen a kiss on the cheek and retired to her bedroom. Topher was contently tucked in a warm, down-filled comforter, feeling its warmth, and reading his latest issue of *Backpacking in New England*.

"Look at this," he said, attempting to show Annie an article about a new kind of hiking boot. There was no response from her. He looked up and saw Annie pulling out a small box from the Norwegian cedar chest that was at the foot of their bed.

Annie sat down beside him on the bed and caressed the hand-painted box decorated with white and pink dogwood flowers. The box, a place for Annie to store her most precious papers, was a gift Topher bought for her at the County Art Show, when they were first married. It now contained the letters addressed to Aspen.

"I think it's time," she said.

Topher noticed the emotion in her words. "Time for what, dear?"

"Aspen's past is somehow connected to the sleigh bell. I can't explain it in words. Call it mother's intuition if you would like, but I just have a feeling."

Topher reached over, took her hand, and kissed it softly. Her warm smile and tear-filled eyes touched Topher's heart. They both knew that Aspen's journey had to begin; a journey that could take him away from the valley, and them.

Topher slipped out of the warm comfort of his bed and walked over to look out the window. "I agree," he said. "Aspen has been inquisitive about a few things lately. Just the other day as we were seeing—you know the thing Aspen and I do together that some people might call meditating—he asked me a strange question. He asked if it was possible for two places to exist at the same time in the same space."

"What was your reply?"

"I told him that I didn't know, and he said nothing further. I felt he really wasn't asking me the question, just voicing his thoughts, and I didn't pursue it. He has asked similar, deep, thought-provoking questions before, but I never have an answer for him. He's just too brilliant for me," Topher said. He took Annie into his arms, pulling her close and hugging her tightly. They clung to each other, both feeling the fear that they might not have much more time with their son. The sleigh bell, apparently, had begun to attract Aspen's attention.

Aspen's Twenty-second Christmas Morning

That night Oreo lay asleep at the foot of his bed. Aspen was awakened by a humming sound that came from the living room. Downstairs he heard the clock cuckooing followed by four dongs.

My twenty-second Christmas morning, Aspen thought as the last dong faded into silence. Again, he heard the faint hum. He gently pulled away the covers, careful not to awaken Oreo. He lowered his bare feet onto the cool pine floor and followed the sound down the stairs to the dimly lit living room.

Through the large picture window, Aspen saw glistening snowflakes reflecting light from the bright moon. "Just like the night I was lost. Thank you," he whispered softly, appreciating the moment of stillness and the beauty of what his eyes were seeing.

The low hum, not unlike the sound of an alpenhorn, was coming from the Christmas tree. He walked over to the fireplace, unlatching the protective screen from its wrought iron hooks, and poked at the small bed of glowing embers; red sparks and puffs of smoke drifted up the chimney. He placed a few pieces of split oak on top of the coals then replaced the screen. The glow from the resurrected flames quickly began to reflect in the many objects around the room. Following the sound, Aspen's eyes came to rest on the sleigh bell. The light from the flames danced upon its surface.

Aspen knelt down in front of the tree and inhaled the scent of pine deep into his chest. He lifted the sleigh bell from the branch that held it. As he did, the humming was replaced by a low vibration.

Aspen jumped as he felt the nudge of Oreo's cold nose against his foot. "What do you make of this?" he asked as he lowered the sleigh bell to her level.

Oreo wagged her tail, lifted her paw placing it on the sleigh bell, and let out a soft playful growl.

"Does it look familiar to you, Oreo? I'm also beginning to remember something."

Bits and pieces of a snowy night, many years ago, began to drift into his consciousness like clouds drifting on slow air currents. The pieces were not of the night when he was lost at the age of ten, but of another time, when he was younger and also lost, but not really lost. He just couldn't put his finger on it.

Aspen placed the sleigh bell around Oreo's neck. "Wanna go for a walk?"

He held onto the sleigh bell as he lifted her so the sound wouldn't wake his parents as he climbed back upstairs to get dressed. Downstairs in the mudroom, he laced up his winter boots, picked up Oreo, stepped out into the snow, and headed for the knoll; there he sat on the cold wooden bench with Oreo contently tucked in his jacket. "Just like old times, wouldn't you agree?" he said to her.

In the distance, he could see the silhouettes of the homes in the valley, soft lights illuminating the windows from within.

"I need to remember," he said as he raised his hands, fingertips touching, palms arched away from each other. As the cold air kissed his face, his thoughts began to drift.

"Something is wakening inside of me, a longing to be somewhere, but I don't know what or where it is. I need to know," he said softly. "We need to know." He gave Oreo a gentle squeeze and headed back to the house to get a few more hours of sleep before Christmas morning arrived.

Aspen's Adoption

Aspen was still sleeping when Oreo wakened to the smell of the bacon coming from the kitchen below.

"Aspen, time to get up," Annie yelled up the wooden stairway that lead to his bedroom loft. Aspen sat up, stretched, walked over to the window, and looked out toward the barren apple trees in the backyard to see if the lone deer had come back to eat the apples he placed on the ground the previous day. To his delight, not only was the doe there, but a friend of hers was too, an eighteen-point buck.

He quickly dressed and ran down the stairs, nearly tripping over Scruff lying at the bottom of the landing. "Merry Christmas, Ma. Anything I can help you with?" Aspen asked as he gave Annie one of his big bear hugs and a kiss on the cheek.

"You can throw a log on the fire and feed your little friend," she said. She smiled at Oreo who was sitting patiently next to her empty bowl.

Topher came through the mudroom door and stomped off the snow from his boots. In one arm was a basket of fresh brown eggs from the henhouse, and in the other arm was a load of firewood. Before opening presents, the Pepins' Christmas tradition was to have a good, old-fashioned breakfast—the kind with fried eggs, pancakes, and Vermont maple syrup.

"Merry Christmas, father," Aspen said. He took the load of wood from Topher's arms and placed it in the firebox that was built into the stone façade of the fireplace.

After breakfast, they retreated to the living room. Aspen stoked the fire. Annie adjusted the old stereo tuning it to NH-Radio, broadcasted from the top of Mount Washington.

"This one is for you," Annie said to Oreo. Annie knew that a new, smelly rawhide dog chew would keep Oreo busy while the family exchanged gifts. Topher received a new pair of hiking boots.

"And you thought I wasn't listening," Annie said, smiling.

Annie's favorite gift was that of a new birdhouse that Topher and Aspen had secretly built together during the summer, hiding it whenever she came into the canoe shop. It was a replica of the old red train depot, which was now the Sip-N-Dip Coffee Shop.

"It is so beautiful. Thank you, both," she said.

Aspen received several items of clothing and a new lightweight easel that he could carry with him when he and his friends went on hiking and canoe trips with GSAC, the Granite State Art Club. After the last gift was handed out, Aspen sat down on the braided rug and placed a big red bow on his head, and then began picking up the discarded wrapping paper.

"You're so silly," Annie giggled. "Don't clean up yet, son; we have one more gift for you."

"Oh," Aspen said, inquisitively raising one eyebrow.

Annie went into the master bedroom, opened the cedar chest, and pulled out the decorated box that contained letters addressed to Aspen. She returned to the living room, sitting down on the rug next to him. She lifted off the box top revealing the stack of letters. Only the first few letters appeared opened. "These are yours," Annie said as she handed them to him.

"My letters?"

"They started coming after your story was printed in the newspaper. Your story about the night you and Oreo were lost in the woods," Annie said.

"They have been coming ever since, and the latest one arrived just this past fall," Topher added.

Aspen looked bewildered as he stared at the pile of letters tied together with an old piece of leather shoe strap.

"We only read the first few that came," said Annie. "They are from people who had similar experiences as you that night in the woods."

"We felt that … we always knew that one day you would seek this mysterious stranger who gave you the sleigh bell instead of helping you safely out of the woods." Annie hesitated for a moment. "Maybe he is a clue to your past."

"My past?" Aspen asked.

Topher sat down on the rug beside Annie. "There's something we have to tell you, Aspen. This is not easy for your mother and me, but we knew that one day we might have to give you an explanation about something. We want you to understand first that parents often have to make choices. Some are very difficult, and what might seem as the right decision at one particular time may not seem like the right decision later."

"Sometimes life wants us to tell a new story, and new decisions need to be made," Annie said.

Aspen felt an overwhelming sensation—a lifting up of sorts, a welcoming of long-awaited answers.

"I have been experiencing some odd things lately. Does this have anything to do with that? Was I abducted?" Aspen said jokingly. He sensed the agony they were feeling. Something was troubling his parents, and he wanted to make it easier for them, whatever it was they were trying to say.

"Not quite," Annie said smiling. Aspen could see the tension tightening the normally soft skin on his mother's face. "When you were lost that night, in the woods twelve years ago, we thought we might never see you again. You see, Aspen, that wasn't the first time you have been lost in the woods." Annie's voice quivered.

"Oh," Aspen said, adjusting himself as Oreo climbed onto his lap. She obviously was going to be part of this family discussion. Aspen gently caressed her back.

"Your mother and I enjoyed hiking and camping in these beautiful mountains when we were first married. Our favorite spot was on Fiddler's Notch, and one year we decided to spend Christmas Eve there. We thought about how wonderful it would be to have a child of our own to share special moments with; for example, camping out under the night sky and watching shooting stars."

"But we were unable to have children, then or now," Annie said.

Annie and Topher sat silently for a moment while Aspen absorbed what had just been said to him. He had a sudden memory of being a little boy, and one morning, while he was feeding the chicks in the henhouse, he asked Annie why he had no brothers or sisters. Her answer had been, "You're all we ever needed," avoiding the question.

"I hear what you're saying, but I don't quite understand," Aspen stated.

Annie continued. "That Christmas Eve night, we heard the sound of bells coming from the forest, a sort of 'ch'ing, ch'ing,' just as you recently have been hearing. We didn't know where the sounds were coming from either and still don't."

"There is a legend called the Legend of Bell Mountain, and it has to do with the sounds of bells," Topher added. "Maybe it's not a legend after all."

"The next morning we heard a child laughing. We thought there must have been other campers nearby. We followed the laughter, only to find a little boy, who was around the age of four. He was all by himself, and there were no signs of anyone else having been there. He was playing with a mountain blue hare under an aspen tree."

They sat in silence, waiting for Aspen to put all the pieces together.

Topher broke the silence. "And that boy was you, Aspen. Long story short, we adopted you. We named you after the aspen tree under which you were playing."

Annie and Topher sat nervously in silence, waiting for Aspen to absorb the fact that they were not his biological parents. Would he be angry or resentful because of the secret kept from him all these years? Would he feel a separation from the people who he thought were his parents? Would he feel rejected because someone else didn't want him? They knew these were questions that adoptive parents often ask themselves, but before they realized it, they had spent too many years pondering, and often the truth goes untold.

"Your mother and I are sure you have lots of questions, but you must believe that we have loved you as our own right from the beginning, and we are truly blessed for having you in our lives," said Topher. "And I am sure there is a good reason for you being left there."

"And a good reason for our finding you as well," Annie added.

Oreo shifted in Aspen's lap and stared at him intensely. It was more than a look; she wanted his undivided attention, and she was trying to communicate something. He remembered that Oreo had been abandoned and left in the shelter. It didn't matter where she came from; what mattered was knowing this little creature loved him unconditionally, even though Aspen was not her original owner.   As he thought this, something miraculous began to happen within Aspen. Instead of confusion, joy began to fill his heart. He didn't know where it was coming from, and he didn't care, and he didn't want the feeling to stop. It was at that moment that he realized Annie and Topher loved him unconditionally as well. This is what Oreo was trying to tell him. Moreover, Aspen was grateful for his parents' love, and for the courage it took to tell their story. He felt no resentment toward them.

"Over the last few months, or more, I have felt there was something more to my life, as if something or someone was beckoning me," Aspen said as he set Oreo on the floor. Annie and Topher stood up, holding each other tightly, afraid he might walk out of their life. What he said next was something they never imagined.

"I love this little dog," he said pointing down at Oreo. "I know this little dog loves me. I see no difference where love comes from, as long as it comes," Aspen had tears in his eyes. They were not tears of sadness, but tears of gratitude, tears of compassion for the two people who loved him as their very own son.

Aspen hugged his parents tightly. "Thank you for the best gift you could have ever given me," Aspen said.

Topher and Annie looked at each other puzzled. "I don't understand," Annie said. "How could this be the best gift ever, and how can you not be hurt or angry with us?"

"You loved me enough to call me your own, and now you love me enough to let me go, if that be the case. How much more can a son ask for?" he said smiling. "This might sound strange, but you have added to who I am, and I'm grateful for it. For a long time now, I thought I was secretly going crazy, but now a weight has been lifted. I had been having dreams of a faraway place. I knew they were real but couldn't prove it and didn't have anyone to share them with. I didn't want you to think I was living in some sort of fantasy land. I was ready to burst open. Now I believe the dreams are pieces of my past." Aspen paused for a moment. "I believe they are pieces of my future as well."

"Aspen, I don't want any one of us to leave this room with any doubts," Topher said. "How can you be so accepting about what you have just been told?"

"As I said, I have always felt there was something—it's hard to find the right words—something out there I am supposed to see, something unknown that I should know, something wonderful. It's all about feelings. You know what I mean?"

"Oh, Aspen," Annie cried as she hugged her son. "We were so afraid to tell you, but truth outweighs everything."

Topher joined in the hug. "We love you, son."

"The bell," Annie said, as she looked toward the Christmas tree where it hung, shimmering with the reflecting lights of red, yellow, blue, and green. "It seems to be a common denominator. The people who sent you the letters also had a visitation by a stranger, and like you, were given a sleigh bell. The original newspaper article written by Mona Foresight from *Say What You Gata Say Gazetteer* is also in the box. It tells about the night you were lost and about the Legend of Bell Mountain. Maybe there is a connection."

"Sleigh bells?" Aspen asked.

"All the people were left with a bell, but unlike the other sleigh bells mentioned in the letters, yours is without a design. It's unique."

Topher continued. "We have heard about other sleigh bells, but yours is the rare one. Your mother and I assumed that your bell is not yet finished," he said with a smile, happy to have found the perfect choice of words. "It's the only reason I can think of that makes sense. I know you have a personal journey to take, a quest."

"I have known there was something special about you right from the start, but especially from the time you were around six years old, if I am remembering correctly. I saw you standing on the knoll facing out into the valley. You were holding your hands together, more like holding something round between your hands. I asked you what you were doing. You never opened your eyes but replied, 'I am listening, would you like to join me?' That is when you, the son, taught me, the father, how to turn inwards. You never knew where you learned that practice."

"I think the best place for you to start is where it began, up on Fiddler's Notch. It seems to be the point of attraction for everything. I can take you there," Topher said excitedly.

"I think that is a good place to start; in fact a great place to start," said Aspen. "But if you don't mind, I'd like to go there by myself and read some of the letters in the meantime, to take it all in. You understand, don't you?"

"Of course we do," said Annie. "Just look for the aspen tree, a very large aspen tree; in fact it's the only one in that area. Next to it you will find a boulder about the size of Cluck's henhouse. It was near there that we found you."

They all looked at each other, each one of them knowing their lives would never be the same again.

Aspen's Quest

Aspen made a light lunch and filled a thermos with hot chocolate. He packed everything in his backpack, along with the bundled letters and some food and water for Oreo. "Let's go, Oreo. We have a hike to take; a quest to go on."

"We'll be home before nightfall," Aspen called to Annie as they headed out the door. He stopped at the canoe shop and picked up the cloth sling used for carrying Oreo when taking her on long hikes. Ambitious as she was, she was so small that she couldn't always keep up with him.

Aspen hiked to the rhythm of his own heart. As he carried Oreo, he felt the warmth of her little body against his chest. He thought about where she came from, who might have lost her, and who could have been the person that had left her at Windblown Animal Shelter.

"First chance we get, we are going to find out where you came from as well," Aspen said to his little friend.

Aspen made his way up to Fiddler's Notch, where his parents said they first found him. "That's odd, it's not far from the very place I was lost when I was ten years old," he said to Oreo. "Let's see if we can find that tree and boulder."

He took Oreo from the baby sling and set her on the snow-covered ground where she stretched and began to root around in the snow.

Aspen had a hunch. He remembered his father telling him about the blue hare he had been playing with on the morning they first found him, and how Oreo had been playing with a blue hare the time he was lost with her. Could both hares possibly be the same? Could there be a connection? Oreo loved to play with Antinelle, her toy rabbit, and she knew the word "antinelle" meant rabbit.

"Oreo, can you find Antinelle?" he asked. Oreo looked up at Aspen, cocked her head to one side, wagged her tail, and then darted off. "She remembers! She remembers!" he shouted stumbling in the snow as he ran after her.

Not far up the hill, they came to a small clearing in the forest. At the edge was an enormous aspen tree and next to it was a large boulder, about the size of the henhouse, just as Annie had described. Sitting at the base was Oreo.

"This must be the place," said Aspen. Oreo wagged her tail, but Aspen wasn't sure why, since there was no rabbit to be found.

He noticed a place in the boulder where a section had been broken off; it was a perfect place to sit and read the letters. Before settling down to read, he took a long piece of rope from his backpack and hooked one end to Oreo's collar and the other to his belt loop.

"Sorry, girl, but I know you; if I don't keep you close, I'll be chasing you down the mountainside," Aspen said with a laugh.

Aspen climbed up onto the rock seat. From his backpack, he pulled out treats for Oreo and the thermos filled with hot chocolate. "Look, Oreo; even a place to set my drink. What more could I ask for?" He withdrew a small pillow for Oreo to sit on in the snow. He tossed her a few chew treats to keep her busy for a while.

As he placed the cup down on the stone armrest, he noticed a small star carved into the rock. He pulled out the old newspaper clipping from his backpack and began to read.

TEN-YEAR-OLD LOST IN TREACHEROUS WAPACK MOUNTAINS ON CHRISTMAS EVE

By Mona Foresight
Ten-year-old Aspen Pepin, a resident of Wapack Valley, was reported missing and presumably lost on Christmas Eve in the treacherous mountains while playing with his little dog, Oreo. Although an initial

search party was organized, efforts to find him were unsuccessful due to nightfall, blizzard-like conditions, and the impenetrable underbrush in the area. The search ended Christmas morning when Mr. Topher Pepin, the boy's father, and good friend, Raulf Ludwig, found little Aspen in an area known to locals as Fiddler's Notch. When asked how he survived the brutal cold night, Aspen stated that during the night he had been visited by a stranger, a man who rode upon a sleigh pulled by what he described as a "funny-looking deer."

"Santa Claus," you might think, but unlikely. The stranger, who has yet to be identified, did not offer any assistance in rescuing the boy. He only offered kind words, inspiring thoughts, and a gift: a sleigh bell. Aspen stated that after the stranger left him, friendly deer came to lie down next to him. The deer kept his body warm and a blue hare kept his head warm.

Could all this be the delusions of a half-frozen boy, or could this be the Legend of Bell Mountain manifesting one more time?

The origins of the legend started here in Wapack Valley, when settlers reported hearing the sounds of bells coming from the mountains. To this day, the source has never been found. The village was often referred to as "Bell Mountain Village," and this became the town's permanent name. Indian folklore also includes similar stories of a "Music Maker in the Mountains," a stranger who helped both Indians and settlers in time of great distress. In every case, the stranger never actually helped anyone, but only offered words of hope and inspiration. The stranger would always leave the same gift: a sleigh bell.

My research throughout the years has produced many similar stories about the stranger. Interestingly, although the stories are similar, the sleigh bells are all different. Diligent research and fieldwork, at my own expense of course, has enabled me to see some of these sleigh bells first hand, and I can tell you that each one is in fact a unique work of art. All the sleigh bells have designs upon them; all designs depict images of the forest, such as leaves, trees, acorns, birds, and animals, but no two are identical.

Aspen took the sleigh bell out of his pocket, wondering why his sleigh bell had no design or markings of any kind. It was completely blank. He read on but kept the vibrating sleigh bell in his hand.

I am sure my readers, as myself, wonder why the stranger in the forest acts in such a manner. Little Aspen stated, "He asked me if I wanted to go home, and he told me to think of good things that reminded me of my mother and father and where I live."

What makes this episode of the legend different is that an additional clue to the stranger's identity was left behind: a gift, not for Aspen, but for his little dog Oreo. It was a star-shaped biscuit. Star-shaped biscuits do show up from time to time, in various places around the valley, but no one knows who leaves them.

So, my dear readers, the legend continues. We wonder how this mysterious stranger is drawn to the people who are in need of help. Why does this stranger help with only words of hope? Where does he go after his visits of encouraging words, and what connection does he have with the animals that show up every time he is near? Why does he leave the gift of sleigh bells? What is the significance of the sleigh bells? We can only wonder. Perhaps this is one legend that we shouldn't solve, but let it live, to learn from it and to acknowledge the example it gives us—to remember what and who means the most to us in our lives.

There is one more note to add to this story: Some older versions of the legend go on to say that the home of the stranger, the bell maker himself, is in fact located right here somewhere in the Wapack Mountain Range. They state that his home is in plain view, but not all can see it. They also state that one day someone will receive a special sleigh bell, a singing sleigh bell, and that person will become "a new maker of bells." What does that mean? I'll leave that one up to your imagination.

Happy Holidays!

The Letters

Aspen pulled out one of the oldest unopened letters sent to him and began to read.

Dear Aspen,

My name is Zephyr Lilly, and I am the great granddaughter of a Native American woman whose name is Breeze. After reading your story in our local newspaper, I began to remember a story that my mother shared with me when I was a little girl. I couldn't remember when exactly that took place, but it did sound similar to yours. One day while canoeing and just enjoying the life of the planet, I felt a cool, gentle wind upon my face, and I remembered. When I arrived home, I found my great-grandmother's journal, flipped through the pages, and found what I was looking for.

When Breeze was a little girl, she also had become lost in the woods, and she describes her story in the old Pennacook Indian language. I have translated it as best as I could. It reads:

*Breeze gathers pinecones from mountain high trail
and lost way. Smoke from fire chase Breeze. Breeze not
see. Smoke on ground and in sky. Breeze cry for help.
Breeze hear sound, new sound, and follow. Breeze see
white man ride deer like horse but not horse. 'Chic-twa
emy ahay?' white man say to Breeze. Breeze not know
man's words but feel what man is asking, "Why Breeze
cry?"*

Breeze must hide from fire.

*Man come down from deer and give Breeze round
gray ball, but not ball for play. Little ball in big ball,
make music. Man smile and say 'Anustayee.' Breeze not
know word but watch man touch head with hand then
touch heart. Breeze do also then understand. Breeze
must trust her heart. Man shake head, yes! Man smile,
and then ride deer away. Breeze remember man's
words. Breeze touch ball to head and to heart and feel
strong. Breeze see cave through smoke. Breeze hide from
fire. Breeze now not afraid. Breeze happy with ball.*

My great grandmother didn't realize her ball
was actually a sleigh bell. As I hold it now, I can
only imagine what she thought of it. Its decorations
are of trees and a pathway, which leads to a village
of Tepees. It is so intricate. If I let my imagination
flow, I could follow the path, right into the village,
and hear the drums of my ancestors. I don't know
if there is a connection to your story, but it sure
sounds like there is one. If you ever want to see the
sleigh bell, just look me up.

Sincerely,

Zephyr Lilly

Aspen was stunned when he read the letter. He knew exactly what
Breeze was saying. Aspen read a few more letters, and although the basic
elements were different, the stories were the same.

"Why is my sleigh bell different, Oreo?" Aspen said aloud. Oreo
gave out a little bark and tugged on the rope indicating she was getting
restless. "I know, Oreo; it's well past noon, and we better get going."

Aspen gave one last look around the area, committing it to memory. "I have a feeling we will be coming back, Oreo, and I think soon, maybe in the spring."

That night Aspen lay in his bed thinking about everything that had transpired in his life: the sounds of his sleigh bell that only he seemed to be able to hear; the realization that he was found by Annie and Topher in the woods as a little boy; and that his experience with the stranger was part of a legend that had been around for generations, maybe even hundreds of years. Yet, he felt okay with it all, even intrigued, knowing there were more pieces to his life than he ever thought. Aspen smiled as he listened to Oreo's snoring and drifted off to sleep.

Oreo's Past

Ever since Aspen had been a little boy, he made time to visit Windblown Animal Shelter during the holidays. Knowing so many animals were alone made him feel sad.

"Oreo, want to go for a ride?" Aspen said. Oreo ran to her toy box next to the front door and pulled out her leash. "What a smart girl you are," he said as they set off toward the shelter.

Mrs. Ogohre used the quiet times of the holidays for completing odd jobs that were too time-consuming any other time of the year. Her first challenge that morning was with a closet of old, outdated files. A smile came to her face as she saw Aspen pulling into the snow-covered parking lot.

The bell above the door announced his arrival. "Hello, Mrs. Ogohre, and a Merry Christmas to you," Aspen said cheerfully, as he went inside.

"And Merry Christmas to you, my dear boy, and to you too, Oreo."

"I should have known that neither, rain, sleet, nor snow would keep you away from here. You are such a dear boy, and I know our boarders will be happy to have some company. They are too often forgotten during the holiday season."

"I agree, Mrs. Ogohre. Besides, Oreo and I have nothing special going on, do we?" he said to Oreo grinning.

"Hmm, I know you better than you think, young man. What are the two of you up to?"

"Oh, nothing much, just enjoying the holiday spirit," he said, placing a bag of dog food on the counter. "Let's go spread some of this holiday cheer," he said and then noticed a small brown bag on the counter. Upon it was the marking of a star. Aspen felt butterflies in his stomach.

"Mrs. Ogohre, where did this come from?" he asked, pointing to the bag on the counter.

"I don't know; the bags just showed up in the donation box. I gave up many years ago trying to figure out who leaves what. You two go on now. As you can see, I have quite a mess going on here. It's the time of year to clean out the cob webs," she said with a laugh.

Aspen pushed on the swinging doors that led to the backroom where the animals were kept. "Hey, little fellow," he said as he scratched a kitten's head through the wire door of the cage. "I am sure you will be going to a new home soon. How could anyone resist a furry little face like yours?"

He noticed the information tag on the cage. It read, "I am going to my new home soon. I have been adopted by the Branhouser family." A smile appeared on Aspen's face.

Aspen made his way through the kennel where he found Old Lucky, a beagle, and the first dog to be placed in the shelter. Mrs. Ogohre had fallen in love with Lucky from the very first moment she laid eyes on him. He had become the mascot of the shelter. He was lucky indeed.

Aspen spent a few minutes with each of the dogs, while Oreo played with some of the puppies. "I think it's time to go, Oreo, or we'll miss Mom's fresh-baked apple pie."

"Do you need any help, Mrs. Ogohre? I have a few minutes I can give you."

"No thanks, child. I'm almost done, but I do have something for you. It's Oreo's original file. Somehow the file was misplaced when you and your father adopted her. I found it while cleaning out the closet."

Aspen noticed the bulge inside the old manila envelope. "What's inside?" he asked.

"Oh, child," she giggled, "I can't remember everything. I'm over twenty-nine, you know."

Aspen opened the envelope and pulled out an old piece of rawhide used as a collar. Attached to it was a small sleigh bell, the size of an acorn.

"Are you all right, Aspen?" Mrs. Ogohre asked as she watched the color drain from his face.

"This is Oreo's?"

"If it's in the envelope, yup, it belongs to her. We don't keep things like that anymore when a stray comes in. It's the room, you know," she gestured as she pointed to the mess in the closet. "Everything we know about her is in the file. Please take it with you. It's yours to keep. I'm only sorry you didn't get it years ago."

Aspen smiled, the color slowly returning to his face, his cheeks regaining their customary rosy blush. "It's okay, Mrs. Ogohre. In fact, this might be perfect timing. Thanks for the file and happy New Year to you."

Mrs. Ogohre smiled as she watched Aspen pull out of the driveway. As she watched snowflakes float slowly to the ground, she couldn't help wondering why he had such a reaction to the bell. "I love this time of year."

Aspen sat in front of the fireplace enjoying the warmth of the fire. He opened the manila envelope containing Oreo's old file.

It read: "Found in woods on morning of October twenty-third near Fiddler's Notch, Wapack Mountain Range by hiker. The identification found on the canine was a rawhide collar. Canine appears to be in excellent health and has an unusually happy disposition. All indications point toward wandering off from owners, however, no homes are located in that particular area. Adoption was made within hours of being delivered to the shelter."

Fiddler's Notch, go figure, he thought, *and she was dropped off the very same morning we adopted her. Just like Oreo, I was found up there, just showing up out of nowhere. Now we both have sleigh bells.*

"Things are getting interesting," he said aloud. "Why would a stranger show up in people's lives and give them sleigh bells, and what does Fiddler's Notch have to do with all this?'

Included in the file was a release form signed by the hiker with a simple scribble resembling a star. Aspen thought about the star that was carved on the boulder where he sat down to read the letters, and the star-shaped biscuit that was left for Oreo by the stranger in the woods. He also recalled the star-stamped paper bags filled with dog biscuits that someone kept leaving around the valley.

"I think we need to take another hike up to Fiddler's Notch," Aspen said. He looked down at Oreo. "What do you think?"

Oreo wagged her tail and barked. "Sometimes I think you understand, and completely!" he said.

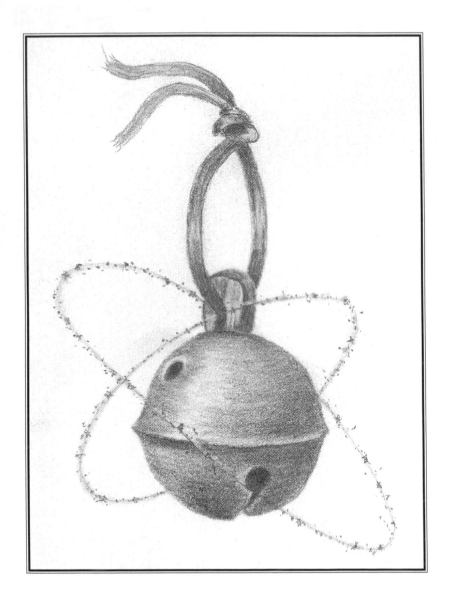

The Passage

The holidays came and went. The beautiful transition between spring and summer unfolded with vibrant splashes of new color, as if an unseen artist had dabbed his brushes of paint on to the living canvas.

Aspen spent many winter nights contemplating what he had learned about himself, and he speculated on how all the stories in the letters were connected to each other. *Is the legend real? It must be real; I'm a part of it myself. Other than some sleigh bells, there is no tangible proof of how I'm connected to this stranger. Why did Oreo and I just drop out of nowhere into the middle of a forest, and not just any forest?*

"The forest, there must be something in the forest," he said aloud. And then it hit him: Aspen remembered his father stating that the animals headed off into the forest, all in the same direction. *Where were they going? There must be something there, something I've overlooked*, he thought.

He went into the kitchen, where his parents were sitting at the table. "I'm going camping tonight," he said. "I think I may have stumbled onto a clue that may link things together. If I head out soon, I will be back up on Fiddler's Notch by this evening and should be back tomorrow afternoon, Sunday at the latest."

Annie, who had been clipping coupons from Friday's newspaper, put the scissors down, giving her full attention to Aspen. "Really, son, what is the clue?" She acted excited for him, but secretly she wished Aspen wouldn't find anything on Fiddler's Notch. She liked things just the way they were.

"This may sound funny, but I think there is some sort of secret passage up there, an unseen opening." Aspen said, gazing out the window toward the mountains. "Father, do you remember when you said all the animals headed off into the forest? Do you know where they went?"

"No, but now that you mention it, it was rather peculiar that they didn't scatter in every direction. They seemed quite unafraid, as if they had completed some assigned task and then returned to wherever they came from."

"Well, there are some clues that keep recurring. On the big boulder where I sat and read some of the letters, I noticed a small star carved into the stone. Raulf said a star-shaped biscuit fell out of my jacket when you picked me up off the ground, the night you found me laying under the pine tree. Someone leaves bags of these biscuits in different places around the valley, including Fifield's Alpine Haus and Windblown Animal Shelter. There's always a star stamped on the bags of treats."

"You're right, son; I never made those connections. You must be on to something".

"And there are the sleigh bells. They have puzzled me for a long time. Everyone who encountered this strange man in the forest received a sleigh bell. What's up with that?" Aspen said, excited with the possibility of a challenge.

"I don't know," said Topher. "What do *you* think?"

"In reading the letters you gave me, I noticed that the designs on the sleigh bells reflect what is spiritually important to the people who received them. The sleigh bells are visual reminders for them, of things that made them happy."

Aspen handed Oreo's sleigh bell to Topher. "Even Oreo's bell has significance. See how the carving shows a pathway into the forest. Maybe that's a way to her former home. Doesn't it look like …?"

"Fiddler's Notch," Topher said, finishing Aspen's sentence.

"What about your sleigh bell, Aspen? Yours is blank," said Annie as she nervously stacked her coupons in a neat pile.

"Not only is it blank, but it makes sounds, sounds only I can hear," said Aspen.

"Oh, what kind of sounds?" Topher asked.

"Of course it jingles when you shake it; but sometimes when it's quiet, and when no one is around, I hear the bell hum like the low tone of an Alpine horn. At first I thought I was going crazy, but if I hold it out and let it hang, I discovered that animals can hear it also. One time, when I was on the mountain, I just put faith into it and allowed it to sing, and the strangest thing happened. Birds began flocking together in the tree branches near me. Deer began to show themselves at the forest's edge, as if they were lured by the sound. There is so much more, but it's hard to put into words."

"Have you figured out why your bell is blank?" Topher asked.

"I'm not sure, Father, but I'm going to find out. I'm close to something—I can feel it."

"Your father and I always felt there was something special about you," Annie said. "Not just because you are our son, but something else, something wonderful and different, is inside of you."

Annie's heart wept silently. She, too, had figured something out. Aspen said his bell sang, and she remembered something that had been written in Mona Foresight's article: "Folklore states that someone will be given a singing bell and become a new bell maker." Could Aspen be the same one in the legend?

That evening, Aspen hiked up into the mountains to the clearing near Fiddler's Notch. He erected his tent in front of the large boulder.

"Just in time to watch the lights come on in the village below," he said to Oreo, and then headed for the ledge that overlooked the valley.

Dusk was a magical time for Aspen. He imagined every light that was turning on as a wish that someone was making.

"There goes a wish, and there goes another one!" he said to Oreo.

The two of them comfortably settled into the small tent, listening to the forest outside whispering its own music.

"Can you hear the crickets, little girl? They are singing you a song," Aspen said. He laughed as Oreo tilted her head, trying to understand. Inside his warm sleeping bag, Aspen drifted off to sleep while being serenaded by the intoxicating sounds of a hoot owl.

In the middle of the night, Aspen was the first to be awakened by the sound of movement just outside the tent. It sounded like a restless horse pacing back and forth. Aspen's heart beat so loudly, he thought that whoever or whatever was outside could hear its pounding. Gathering up his courage, he worked himself out of the sleeping bag and crawled to the front of the tent. He looked out through the screen, and in the moonlight, he was able to make out the silhouette of a rider upon a large animal, a horse perhaps. It snorted, and Aspen realized it was not a horse at all.

Oreo barked and scratched against the tent screen, her tail wagging.

"Shhh, little one, now is not the time," the stranger outside whispered softly.

Was he talking to Oreo or the animal he was riding? Aspen wondered. *And why was Oreo acting like that just looking out, wagging her tail instead of barking?*

In just a moment, Oreo apparently reached some kind of conclusion about the stranger. She contently sat down.

"Tut-tut." The stranger gave his command and pulled away, vanishing into the forest.

The tranquil sounds of the forest returned. Aspen sat in silence, goose bumps running up and down his body.

"That was him, the stranger. I know it was; I can feel it, I'm close," he whispered.

Somehow Aspen managed to fall back asleep. The next morning Aspen put on his hiking boots and stepped outside the tent. "What a beautiful morning," he said aloud as he stretched. He had momentarily forgotten about the visitation during the night, that is, until he saw the deer tracks on the ground. Once again he felt goose bumps dancing upon his skin. Kneeling down, he placed his hand in one of the tracks. He saw that they led in the direction of the forest.

"Okay, Oreo, first thing's first; let's get some breakfast. Do you agree?"

Oreo wagged her tail in anticipation.

"Dry food for you and a couple of granola bars for me."

As Oreo ate her food, Aspen poured a pouch of instant hot chocolate into the pot of boiling water sitting in the hot coals of the campfire. He stood up and stepped into the center of the hoof tracks. He took a step forward, and then he followed another, and kept following the tracks until he came to the edge of the clearing. He couldn't believe what his mind was telling him, but he could believe what his eyes were showing him. The tracks ended abruptly at the edge of the clearing, disappearing into thin air. He turned around to make sure he was reading the tracks right. They came from the forest through the clearing and then vanished into nowhere.

Something is here, I just know it, and I can feel it, he thought. *It's a way to something or somewhere, a passage.*

He thought about all the clues and remembered the star carved on the hand rest of the boulder and decided to examine it further. He climbed up on the boulder and sat in the chair looking at the star. *This must be here for a reason,* he thought, and as he sat there, an idea came to him. He rubbed the star with his palm. Nothing happened—no magical genie, no lightning bolts, and no smell of roses. He laughed at himself for being so silly.

Oreo had finished eating and was now sitting at the rope's end, staring. She turned to gaze at Aspen with a beckoning look, and then she looked back to the edge of the clearing where the tracks ended.

Aspen examined the star and on impulse, rubbed it just for good luck. He jumped off the boulder, and then he walked over to Oreo. "What do you see that I can't, Oreo?" he said, kneeling down beside her and scratching her behind her ear.

The jingle of Oreo's sleigh bell on her collar gave Aspen an idea. He knelt down in front of Oreo and looked closely at the scene on her bell. It looked just like the area he was standing in, including the boulder and path leading to the edge of the clearing.

Maybe my sleigh bell is a key, Aspen thought. He crawled back into the tent, digging through his backpack until he found it. He untied Oreo's rope from where it had been attached to her collar. He picked her up and held her close to him. "Are you ready?" he whispered into her ear.

Aspen walked into the middle of the clearing and faced the edge of the forest where the tracks disappeared. He stretched out his hand letting the sleigh bell drop and hang from its leather strap. It immediately began to hum, softly at first and then louder. It began to shimmer, and shooting stars, no bigger than a pinhead, circled around it at great speed. The forest in front of him mimicked the sleigh bell and shimmered as well. Suddenly, the trees seemed to shift their position. Aspen's heart pounded.

"There it is!" he shouted. "I knew it, a passage!"

Where the deer tracks ended, the trees had separated, revealing a path that led into a grassy meadow. It was one of the most beautiful meadows he had ever seen. Purple and yellow lupines were blooming everywhere. Acres and acres of wild flowers painted the meadow with their colors, and the air was heavy with their scent.

It was a gift, an invitation for anyone with true intensions and who was pure of heart.

The Meadow

Aspen, with Oreo at his side, walked forward slowly. He turned to see the trees guarding the entrance to the meadow that was closing behind him.

"We better leave something behind to find our way back," he said. He knelt down and slipped off his boots and socks. "This feels better." He wiggled his toes on the soft grass. "If you don't take off your shoes once in a while and go barefoot, the world will always feel like a piece of leather beneath your feet. Don't you agree, Oreo?" He set the pair of boots to one side of the path as a marker.

Karner Blue butterflies played a game of touch-and-go, welcoming him and landing on his head as he walked beside a weathered split-rail fence that led to the summit of a hill. The immensity of the green lush meadow that lay before him overwhelmed his senses. Aspen looked back toward the passageway. "This meadow is ten times bigger than the Wapack Valley, yet here it is, two places in one place. How can that be?"

He was struck by an unmistakable feeling of recognition. Was it déjà vu, or had he really been to the stone cottage nestled in the middle of the meadow before?

Oreo, ran ahead of him, then turned around and ran back to Aspen, barking as if urging him to hurry.

"You know this place, don't you?" Aspen picked up his little friend and gave her a hug. "Not too fast now," he said, setting her down. He watched as she ran down the grassy path toward the cottage. She seemed to know just where to go, just as she did the very first day she had been brought home from the shelter. Could this be her home, the place from where she wandered away?

Attached to the red carriage barn was a small workshop. Its stone chimney gave off puffs of cotton like smoke. Inside, a workbench was located next to a window that looked onto the meadow. On the bench were two tree branches, about a foot and a half long, positioned so that the branches formed an A-frame. Suspended in the center of the frame was a partially completed sleigh bell.

At the workbench sat Iver, gazing at the bell and seemingly deep in thought. Although his hair was white, it was impossible to discern his age. A few strands of blondish hair hinted of earlier days; his smooth skin was that of a thirty-year-old, and his sky blue eyes sparkled with the imagination of a child. He was carving a scene into the new sleigh bell, and yet his workbench was void of any tools. Only a plate of partially eaten cookies and a cup of hot chocolate sat upon it.

Iver closed his eyes and simply thought about the beautiful images he wanted to impress upon the bell. As he imagined a scene, it appeared on the bell.

A broad smile came to his face when the barking of a dog and the jingling of a sleigh bell interrupted his concentration. "Oreo," he said, joy radiating from his face as he looked out the window and saw her running down the hill. He stood up, took off his leather apron, and tossed it on the bench. The screen door squeaked as he pushed it open.

"Oreo, my sweet Oreo. You have come home to Papa!" He bent down and Oreo jumped into to his waiting arms. He stood up and spun around, dancing. "Oreo, at last; we have been waiting many years for you to return. It always seems so long when you leave," he said to her, hugging her once more before setting her on the ground.

Oreo, her tail wagging, turned, her nose pointing up the hill. Iver followed her gaze. There on top of the hill stood Aspen. The two men stared at each other.

Aspen couldn't believe his own eyes, as he recognized the face of the man. He was the same man who had helped him in the forest when he was lost as a child. Not only that, he was sure that this person was the same person he had heard in the forest last night.

Iver, exhilarated, looked upon the face of this young man, his son.

Believing

Aspen walked slowly, methodically down the path. The tickling blades of soft grass beneath his feet conjured up faded memories of playing here when he was a child. The sensation of him being here before was growing.

The reindeer, he thought, *are they still in the field?* He looked to his right, and his intuition was confirmed; they were there. *I must have been here before, otherwise how could I have known that?!*

Even at fifty feet away, Aspen could see Iver's smile. Iver then put his hands together, fingertips touching and palms slightly apart, just the way Aspen had often stood with Topher on the knoll behind the canoe shop. Iver stayed in this posture until they were standing face to face.

"Welcome home, son."

Aspen was overwhelmed by a wave of recognition. He smiled, speaking just two words. "Iver, father!"

Iver reached out, pulling Aspen close to him, hugging him. "Welcome home, son," he repeated. Tears of immense joy ran down his cheeks, and his heart pounded so hard he had difficulty talking. "We have much to talk about, and I am sure you have many questions; but first, before you say anything, I want you to look at your sleigh bell."

Puzzled, Aspen pulled out the sleigh bell from his pocket and offered it to his father.

"No, you hold it. Let it hang, and turn it slowly," Iver said.

Aspen held the sleigh bell and twisted the strap slowly between his fingers. As the sleigh bell turned, an image of the meadow, cottage, barn, and workshop began to magically emerge in the gray metal. Even the delicate details of lupine and deer in the field were forming.

"Yes, Aspen, this is your home," said Iver.

They were interrupted by Oreo's barking, as she ran up to the cottage door.

"Oreo misses Elta's good cooking," Iver said, rubbing his belly.

"Elta! My mother?" Aspen asked.

"Why of course, your mother!" Iver snickered.

Aspen chuckled. "I suppose I should have guessed."

"Well, I'm sure you have many questions to ask, but I know both you and Oreo must be hungry," Iver said. "First we will eat, and then we will sit by the fire and talk. Is that okay with you?"

"Of course," Aspen answered.

"Good! Then Oreo and I will go help Elta inside. You walk around, reacquaint yourself with the place. Go anywhere, look into anything, explore, and don't forget to acknowledge your feelings. Remember, this is your home."

Before Aspen could ask Iver what he meant, Iver took Aspen's backpack and walked toward the stone cottage where Oreo sat patiently by the front door.

Aspen closed his eyes, and a gentle breeze scented with lilac caressed his face. He stood in silence trying to understand what it was that he was experiencing. Was it real, or was he dreaming it all? He didn't know where to begin.

His thoughts were interrupted by strange sounds coming from behind him. He hesitated to turn around. Whatever it was, it was breathing warm air down the back of his neck.

"Okay, there is nothing bad in this place," he said to reassure himself. Slowly he turned, coming nose to nose with an unusually large reindeer.

"Jiminy Cricket!" he screamed, stumbling backward and falling on his rump. The reindeer grunted several times and shook its head.

"You're laughing at me, aren't you?" The reindeer grunted again. Aspen thought he saw a hint of a grin. "It can't be; reindeer can't smile." The deer gestured with its head for Aspen to follow as it turned and started walking back through fields of unparalleled beauty. It occasionally dropped his enormous head, rubbing its wet nose against the flowers, and each time it looked back at Aspen, as if he was teaching him to recognize the smallest things this meadow had to offer.

Finally, the reindeer stopped, turned to face Aspen, and walked toward him. It came close, looking right into his eyes. Aspen stared into the reindeer's chestnut eyes and suddenly remembered. "Windwalker! It's you!" Memories of riding on Windwalker's back as a little boy came back to him. "My friend; my dear old friend." He reached up and placed a hand on each side of Windwalker's head, and then placed his forehead against the reindeer's. They stood there in silence, both rekindling their connection, their friendship, absorbing the presence of each other.

Aspen was startled by a low rumbling sound in the distance. It began coming closer, and the ground started vibrating beneath his feet. His mouth opened in astonished wonder as a group of reindeer came running toward him.

"Yahoo, yahoo!" Aspen shouted as they approached. He laughed with joy and reached out to touch many of them as they surrounded him. He called out to many of them by name: "Morning Star, Canyon Jumper, Butterfly, and Rosebud."

Aspen knew that they came to welcome him home. He turned to face Windwalker. "Thank you, Windwalker; you helped me to remember." Windwalker grunted, giving Aspen a nudge with his nose. His job for now was complete.

Aspen walked back to the barn and slid open the large door that rolled on iron tracks. Inside were several wooden wagons and sleighs. Among them, the pale blue sleigh in which he had seen Iver. It looked brand new, and yet he knew that it had to be extremely old. As he approached, the bells began to vibrate. "Every one of you is a gift of hope for someone in need," he said with a smile.

On the left side of the barn was a pair of swinging doors leading into Iver's workshop. To the right of the doors hung a small, painted plaque that read: "In Optimism There Is Magic."

He entered the unusual workshop. It seemed like a comfortable den, with a braided rug in front of an open fireplace. The smell of burning wood was comforting, reminiscent of his home with Topher and Annie. There were numerous shelves filled with books with binders of many colors. Three fiddles of various sizes hung on the wall over the fireplace mantle. Next to the window was the workbench, and upon it the tree branch holder that housed a partially completed sleigh bell. Aspen took the sleigh bell out of the stand and held it in his palm. It vibrated ever so softly. "And who will you be helping?" Aspen said. He replaced the bell in its holder.

Aspen sat in the rocking chair adjacent to the fireplace and stared into the mesmerizing flames, listening to the crackle of the burning logs. It felt like home.

He closed his eyes, taking pleasure in the quiet moment. When he opened his eyes, he noticed photos neatly arranged on the mantle. They were of young people, both boys and girls. Aspen stood, walked over to the pictures, and looked at them closely. Some of the pictures looked old, very old indeed. Some were just simple sketches dated in the eighteen hundreds. Some of the posers were holding their hands in the same position he used when he was listening. Aspen felt something stir within him. Could they be relatives, maybe even his brothers and sisters? Aspen chuckled to himself. The list of questions he had to ask Iver just grew by a few more.

Aspen looked back into the workshop before letting the doors swing back into place. He read the sign once more and smiled.

Aspen opened the cottage door. As he entered, he smelled the aroma of Elta's apple pie baking in the oven. Oreo came to greet him, wagging her tail as she always did. He picked her up, and she licked his face. "I haven't been gone that long," he said, laughing. As he held her, he felt a new sense of gratitude and love for her.

Aspen stood in the doorway of the old kitchen and noticed a cookie sheet filled with star-shaped dog biscuits. "Aha, that's where they come from," he said aloud.

Elta turned, hearing his voice, and went over to hug him, and held him tightly.

Her eyes sparkled as only a mother's could. "Aspen, my dear son! You haven't changed a bit. I would know you anywhere, even if you don't fully remember me. Don't worry, Aspen, everything will come back to you swiftly now that you are home."

He sat down at the table rubbing his hands in the wide groove where the wood was worn away from generations of plates being set there.

"That was your favorite spot when you were just a little boy," Elta said with a broad smile. She took the perfectly browned apple pie out of the cast-iron stove and placed it on a round piece of soapstone in the center of the table. Iver made peanut butter and strawberry preserve sandwiches, Aspen's favorite, and neatly stacked them on a plate decorated with periwinkles.

"I have some questions …," Aspen started to say, but he was immediately interrupted.

"Not now, first we will eat," Elta said with a firm voice followed by an amazingly warm smile.

Iver chuckled, "She has someone new to pester now."

They sat there in silence looking into each other's eyes. Sometimes words were not necessary to generate feelings of love.

After eating, they retired to the cozy living room. Oreo was fast asleep in front of the fireplace, snoring. Aspen wondered why there was a fire burning in the fireplace this time of year. It wasn't cold outside, but maybe it was for ambiance.

"And your first question?" Iver asked.

Aspen chuckled. "There are so many. Let's start with Oreo. My father and I …," Aspen started to say but stopped, realizing he now had two fathers.

"Annie and Topher are your parents also, through pure, unconditional love," said Iver. "Never stop calling them your parents. You just have to get use to the idea of having more than two."

"My father and I found Oreo at Windblown Animal Shelter," Aspen said.

"I brought her to the shelter that very morning knowing you would find each other. It's her joy and her job to be with you. Then when the right time came, she helped you find your way home, sometimes giving you clues, like staring off into the forest, and at times tilting her head to indicate that she really might understand what you were talking about. You see, Aspen, Oreo has the great attribute of having the heart and mind of a puppy. She was not supposed to get you lost in the woods when you were ten years old. Your time was still a few years off. She just likes to chase things. But it always works out. It's all good. No one ever comes home before they are ready. Do you understand, Aspen?"

Elta reached over and gently grasped Aspen's hand. "Iver, I don't think Aspen does."

"Oreo is a genuine guide dog; the real McCoy you might say,

always guiding someone. She always was, and always will be; as long as you believe, she never ages," said Iver.

Aspen looked at Oreo and smiled warmly as he pondered what Iver just told him. "I think I do understand. But what about me? Annie and Topher found me as a small boy lost in the woods when I was around four years old."

Iver laughed so loudly that he awakened Oreo. "You were not lost, my boy, and you never will be truly lost or alone." Iver explained. "If you can think back to that day, you were never sad or frightened, were you? I kept a watchful eye on you and so did your animal friends. I left you there knowing the Pepins would find you. You see, Aspen, it was time for you to leave this meadow for a while, to experience and have life lessons in a world that is full of contrasts; a world full of wonder and, most of all, love in its many facets."

"It's normal not to fully remember this place or us, but you are never truly cut off from remembering," Elta said, smiling.

"Have you ever thought about where you learned to listen or wonder why you say 'thank you' aloud whenever you see beautiful things?" Iver asked.

"No, but other people have, including my father. I taught him to meditate, but we never used that word for some reason. We simply called it listening. We often listened on the knoll behind our home."

"We call it listening because that is what you are doing—just being quiet, enabling you to hear what you normally can't. Topher is a wonderful human being and very keen to his inner senses, and so is Annie," Iver explained. "They couldn't have children of their own. Their wanting is what we felt, and we knew they would be loving parents, so they were chosen to be yours."

Aspen was silent. Iver could sense what he was feeling and thinking. "You are wondering how you can be our child when we are so old. You saw the other children, your siblings in the photographs in the workshop, yes?"

Aspen picked up Oreo, placed her in his lap, and stroked her soft fur. "Yes, I did, and that question has crossed my mind."

"I can't exactly explain all of it to you, Aspen. Sometimes events outshine words. We are quite old, you know," Iver said, laughing. "We only have a faded recollection of the very past."

"You know what they say about older people," Elta said with a giggle.

Iver continued. "One day as a young couple, Elta and I were walking through the forest that is now called Fiddler's Notch. Somehow we came upon the passage and walked through it onto the same grassy path you walked down today. That was many years ago, Aspen, uncountable years. This beautiful, remarkable meadow felt quite familiar to us, as if we too were returning home. In fact, we used to imagine a place such as this when we were just courting."

"It's a magical meadow, you know," Elta said.

"This was all here, the cottage, the barn, and the workshop, just kind of waiting for us, and we felt right at home. Oreo was here, and of course we just had to stay and take care of her," said Iver. "At first we were bewildered, as you might imagine, just as you are now, but then a certain clarity came to us. We were instantly filled with joy and gratitude to have found this place. We never looked back."

Iver gazed around the cottage. "There have been a few upgrades since that time," he said jokingly. "I began to make sleigh bells as a hobby. One day while I was sitting at my workbench, deciding on how I could decorate one of them, I somehow sensed that someone on the other side of the passageway needed help. The sensation was so strong and vivid that I got up and went outside, expecting to see something. When I came back to the bench, a design had appeared on the bell, and I recognized the general area. It was a cave formed by an ancient rockslide, a very dangerous place. I sensed it had caved in on some explorers, a family looking for shelter, and I was correct. I grabbed the sleigh bell, knowing it would guide me to exactly where they were. When I found them, I realized I couldn't help them because the boulders were too massive.

"I didn't know what to do, but then I felt the sleigh bell vibrating in my pocket. I have to admit, it scared me the first time that happened. When I pulled out the bell, I noticed the scene had changed. It showed an opening on the other side of the mountain. As soon as I saw this, I knew there was a way out for them.

"'Please help us, we want to get out,' they screamed. That's when I got the idea of giving them the sleigh bell. I knew I couldn't divulge who I was or where I came from. I told them that they needed to calm down while the dust settled. I began asking them questions: who they were, where were they going, and what was important to them. I gave them words of encouragement and explained it was not safe to breathe the dust by talking anymore. Instinctively, I slid the sleigh bell through a narrow opening and left. As the dust settled, enough light came through the opening for them to see the design on the sleigh bell. They found their way out through the back of the cave."

"That's when the Legend of Bell Mountain was born," Elta said.

"It has been like that ever since," Iver continued. "I always know ahead of time when someone will need a bell. Somehow I get impressions about the people I am going to help, where they live, for example, and I visually carve these places of importance onto the sleigh bells, which makes each one unique."

"It's a gift," Elta said with pride.

Aspen scratched his head, trying to make sense of what they were saying.

"I give the sleigh bells to people who find themselves in situations where they feel there is no way out," Iver continued. "Later on, the sleigh bells remind them that any unwanted situation they might find themselves in can be made better. All they have to do is start where they are and think of what they want most, nothing more. Receiving a sleigh bell gives them hope and causes them to find the inner strength that is inside every one of us. None of the sleigh bells have any magical powers by themselves, but the fact is that any situation will improve, if you believe they will."

"But my sleigh bell was blank; at least it was until I arrived here, and then it magically changed," Aspen said.

"I stand corrected," Iver said. "Almost none of the sleigh bells have magic. The magic is within us, though, not in the sleigh bells. I believe you have already figured this out. You will also learn how to make sleigh bells, Aspen; for you are also a bell maker. I know it's not easy to believe at first. You also will be a giver of hope. You see, I do make sleigh bells as a hobby; for example, to decorate the harnesses on the sleighs. Every few years, one will refuse to keep its design. If I start one, and the next day all the images have disappeared, I know that a new bell maker is to be born. It's at that time that I go looking for Oreo to let her know she will have another child to guide. I always find her hanging around with Windwalker. I bet you have memories of riding Windwalker, yes?"

"Yes, Windwalker helped me to remember those things this

morning. And are you saying that when we are four years old, we leave here to learn and experience the world?" Aspen asked.

"No," Elta answered. "Not all children leave at the same time. It depends on their needs and desires, but I have to say that the time we have together is always too short of a period."

"Where are all my siblings?" Aspen asked, thinking about the photographs in the workshop and on the bookshelf.

"They are everywhere in the world, wherever they are needed," she proudly answered.

Aspen's thoughts returned to Annie and Topher. "Am I needed somewhere other than in the Wapack Valley?" he asked.

Elta and Iver knew what emotions Aspen was feeling inside.

"Yes," Elta softly replied. "You are needed somewhere else, perhaps far from here and perhaps far from your home in the valley, and from Annie and Topher."

"Won't they be lonely?" Aspen said in a near-whisper.

He held Oreo a little bit tighter, feeling torn between the inevitable; torn between excitement for himself and sadness for the Pepins.

Iver reached over and placed a hand on Aspen's shoulder, comforting him. "Don't be sad, Aspen. It's not as you think. Much happiness awaits you and the Pepins. You can explain everything to your mom and dad, and they are always welcomed to visit you, wherever in the world you might be. We knew long ago that Annie and Topher were loving and honest people, always true to their word and would never divulge the … all of this," Iver said, extending his hands. "And you can visit them anytime you feel like it, just like any son should who has moved away from his home. You can also visit us anytime in an instant."

"But, father, how can I do that if I am to be so far away?"

Iver felt a ping of joy hearing Aspen call him father. It had been a long time.

"The same way you came here, silly boy." Iver held up his hand, pretending he was holding Aspen's sleigh bell, shaking it. "Just believe and feel what's in your heart, and incredible things will be open to you, so wondrous you will be hard to find words to describe them."

"There is one thing that, well … troubles me."

"What is that, Aspen?" asked Elta.

Aspen lifted Oreo and kissed her on her head.

Spoken words were not needed here; Iver and Elta could see the devotion Aspen had for his Oreo. They didn't know what to say. Even though they had been through this same situation before, somehow it was different with Aspen. A new outcome seemed inevitable, but they didn't know what that would be.

Iver went to Elta and hugged her close. The silence in the room felt heavy.

Aspen held Oreo tightly as though someone was going to rip her out of his arms. He stared intently into his father's eyes. Then suddenly, Aspen smiled broadly. He had a hunch and was going to put it to the test.

Iver scratched the side of his cheek. "What are you smiling about?"

Aspen placed a finger up to his lips, indicating they should listen.

They remained silent as Aspen closed his eyes and breathed deeply. He exhaled slowly, and as he did, a sound of scratching was heard at the door.

"What's that?" Iver asked as he released his hold on Elta. He opened the door, glancing back at Aspen who was now grinning from ear to ear. Iver opened the door. He looked down to see a small brown and white dog.

"Well, who are you, little fellow?" Iver asked as he picked up the bundle of fur. Iver laughed as the little dog wagged its tail while offering him wet kisses on his cheeks.

"You just have to name her," Aspen said.

Iver turned to look at Aspen. Unbelievable joy and pride filled his heart. For the first time, one of his children had a solution for the heartbreaking problem of having to leave Oreo behind. None of his children ever wanted to leave her, but only Aspen had the unwavering desire, a determination to find an answer. He was unlike any other: unique, wise and quick to learn.

"Just believe and feel what's in your heart and incredible things will be open to you, so wondrous it will be hard to find words to describe them," Aspen said, repeating Iver's words. "Remember the secret of the sleigh bell."

Return to Wapack Mountain

Annie and Topher sat quietly on the bench that overlooked the valley. Aspen had only been away since the previous morning, but it seemed like a week. They wondered what Aspen might have found on his journey, and if he would return. Annie worried for Topher. His normally erect posture was now limp, and his face was strained, reflecting his pain.

Topher stood up and walked over to the edge of the knoll. The lights in the village below were just starting to twinkle in the distance. He placed his hands together, fingertips touching, palms slightly apart, and he began to breathe deeply. Annie sat in silence and watched him, just as she had done many times before. Every breath seemed to be renewing him.

Their shared silence was broken by the faint sound of a bell, a sleigh bell. They both turned around to see Oreo bouncing up the path.

"Oreo," Annie shouted, reaching down to pick her up. Not far behind her was Aspen. Topher walked over to Aspen, looked into his eyes, and hugged him tightly.

"Welcome home, son. We were getting worried," he said, trying to hold back his tears.

"Oreo and I are both fine," Aspen said smiling. He walked over to Annie and gently hugged her.

"You both need to sit down. I have an incredible story to tell you. I found the passage, a sort of gateway, and it's magical."

"Oh," Topher said.

Aspen knelt in front of them and began to tell his story. "During the night, someone was riding what I thought was a horse around my campsite. I was a little rattled, but Oreo seemed to recognize the stranger outside. The next morning I saw deer tracks disappearing into the edge of the forest—and I do mean disappearing."

"Who was it, Aspen?" Topher asked.

"I'll get there," Aspen said excitedly. "I remembered the stories of the blue hare when I was apparently lost in the woods on two separate occasions, and I remembered what you said father, that the animals always returned into the forest together and always in the same direction."

"That's true, Aspen; I had forgotten about that."

"I remembered that Oreo liked to play with her toy rabbit, Antinelle." Aspen reached down, lifted Oreo from Annie's lap, and raised her high in the air. "I had a hunch. I asked her if she knew where Antinelle was, and she apparently did. She ran to the edge of the clearing where we were camping, and she started barking at what I first thought was nothing. It was then that I knew something was there, but what? Then an idea came to me—the sleigh bell."

"What do you mean, Aspen?" Annie asked.

"Remember I said my sleigh bell sometimes sings?"

"I do," she replied. "And you heard some sort of bell sound at the tree lighting ceremony. I wanted you to believe that it was your imagination. Truth be known, I never did want you to find anything that would take you away from me. I'm sorry."

"That's okay, Ma, really."

Aspen continued. "I held the sleigh bell in the air, and it started to hum, louder than it had ever before, as if it was singing. Then the edge of the forest began to shimmer, sort of evaporating away, and a passageway appeared. Beyond the passage was a meadow, a blooming meadow with fields of Lupine of every color. Other flowers are growing there as well, and the smell of lavender was so strong it came right through to where I was standing."

Annie and Iver looked at each other blank-faced.

"I know, it's hard to believe, but if you don't believe that, you will never believe the rest," Aspen said with a laugh. "I walked through the passageway, straight into the meadow. I followed an old fence next to a path that led me to a stone cottage."

Aspen paused for a moment for Annie and Iver to mentally follow him. "I know, it sounds unbelievable, but it is true. I can prove it to you, and I will."

"We know you wouldn't lie, Aspen," Topher said.

"There is more, much more!" Aspen said.

The day was nearly gone. The dark sky put on a brilliant display of twinkling stars. Bell Mountain Village lay perfectly silent; its lights flickered in the cool night air.

Annie and Topher waited for Aspen to continue. He seemed nervous and fidgeted. "What is it?" Annie asked.

"I found them ... my parents." Aspen paid close attention to Annie's reaction. She flinched. Aspen decided to wait for her to speak.

"Are they good people?" Annie finally asked.

Aspen kneeled down in front of Annie and held her warm hands. "Yes, they are wonderful people. Her name is Elta, and his name is Iver," he said, looking at Topher. "They love me, as both you do. It wasn't easy for them to let us go."

"Us? What do you mean by us?" Annie asked.

"Why Oreo, of course; she belongs to them, to me now. We were set up, Father. Iver left Oreo at Windblown Animal Shelter knowing we were going to find her. Imagine that!"

Again, Annie and Topher were silent.

"I told you this would be hard to believe. The Legend of Bell Mountain is real. Iver and Elta are part of the legend people have been speaking about for all these years. I am also part of it. I am also to be a stranger that helps people. I am also to be a bell maker. I was placed in the forest to be found, set free you might say; to gain some experiences of life, to know what love is, especially unconditional love. That is where you two came in. You adopted me and loved me as your very own, unconditionally. Unconditional love is what I personally was to experience."

Annie's voice quivered. "I am sure there is much more to explain Aspen, but for now, just answer one question for me.

"Sure, Ma, what is it?"

"Will you be leaving us?"

Aspen stood up and took a deep breath. "For years I have had this sensation of being pulled, a yearning to go somewhere, but I never knew what or where it was. I, like other bell makers, am needed all over the world. There are many such places as the meadow, but not all are the same, and not all are near here." Aspen turned so that his parents could not see the grin on his face. "Iver and Elta said I am needed far away." Aspen then turned to face them, still restraining his grin. He paused for a moment to add some drama to his story. "But they want me to stay here, right here in our valley," Aspen said and began to laugh.

Annie stood, and Topher held her close.

"It seems that my belief in Iver and Elta has set them free. They told me they were ready to move on, although they didn't elaborate on what that meant. They have been waiting for someone to take over for them, right here in Fiddler's Notch, if someone could and wanted to. And I do. So you see, I won't be that far away after all."

He walked over to his parents and hugged them both, his heart filled with love for them.

"I have taken the same path as my brothers and sisters before me. We have all learned from our experiences, but I believed where the others could not. I learned that if one just believes and feels what's in their heart, then all things would be open to them. I have learned the secret of the sleigh bell."

"And what is the secret, Aspen?" Annie asked.

"Except for the sleigh bells that are given to new bell makers, there is no magic in them, but they are symbols that stimulate people to use their minds in order to follow what's in their hearts, be it an immediate solution giving hope when they feel there is none to be found, or to future desires.

"For example, people believe that sleigh bells caused words of encouragement to come true, but in actuality, it is their own belief that makes something come true."

Aspen continued. "As for me, I believed my sleigh bell held a clue to my past and future. Truth be known, it wasn't the sleigh bell that led me on my personal path; it was what was already in my heart. All sleigh bells help us in many ways, including our own unique paths.

"The secret to the sleigh bell is that it will help you to believe in your desires, your dreams and goals, whatever it is that you want, and to believe in a little magic. Soon you will discover that all the magic comes from within. That is the secret of the sleigh bell."

PASS IT ALONG

As I have often done with puzzles and books that I have completed, I sign the box or book, along with adding the date and the place where I currently live. Then I pass it along to someone else and ask him or her to continue the practice. If you enjoyed *The Secret of the Sleigh Bell*, please think about whom else might enjoy reading it. Who knows what might be passed on to you!

_____

_____

_____

_____

_____

_____

_____

_____

_____

_____

_____

_____

_____

_____

_____

_____

_____

_____

_____

_____

_____

_____

_____